The Legend of Anadulan

By Joelle Davis

This is a work of fiction. Similarities to real people, places, or events are entirely coincidental.

THE SECRET OF ANADULAN

First edition. November 19, 2023.

Copyright © 2023 Joelle Davis.

ISBN: 979-8223790952

Written by Joelle Davis.

Table of Contents

"God is our refuge and strength, an ever-present help in trouble."
Psalm 46:1

Chapter 1

"...Happy Birthday to you!" The chorus of childish voices turned into giggles as Hannah Joy Weaver took in a huge breath to blow out her candles. After she successfully blew them out, everyone at her party cheered for her and scrambled to get a piece of the beautiful cake. Hannah's mother had bake it and frosted it herself with Hannah's help. The frosting was a creamy white and had been placed in swirls across the top of the cake. Her mother had told her that the cake matched her party dress. The dress was white silk with swirls of white tulle that looped along the waist of her skirt. A white satin bow tied up half of her light blonde curly hair that hung down to her waist. Her sky-blue eyes were a stark contrast to the white and made her look a bit angelic.

Hannah was ten years old now, and her parents had arranged for a special party. Her friends from school, Lottie and Samantha were there, along with her three cousins, Aunt and Uncle, and her beloved Grandfather Charles. Grandfather was Hannah's favorite person to be around. He would make her laugh with his silly stories, and he would dance with her. But the best was when he would tell stories about when he was an explorer. He would capture her attention with his tales about dragons and snakes, storms and wild seas, and most importantly, unicorns. Hannah's mother and father told her that there were no such things as unicorns, but Hannah believed that they were real with her whole heart.

Hannah's father, Steven Weaver, was a wealthy merchant who shipped in goods from far and wide to the Island of Anadulan. Julia Weaver, his wife and Hannah's mother, was a true lady, kind, gentle, and exquisitely lovely in all her ways. They all lived together in a rather large house by the Connema sea. It was filled with wonderful things from all over the world. Her father had to travel quite often and would bring back the most beautiful things for Hannah and her mother. Hannah hated when he was away, but she knew he would always come back.

"Hannah, would you like some cake?" Her mother asked.

Hannah smiled widely and replied, "Yes please!".

Her mother chuckled and placed a slice of the cake onto a plate before handing it to her. Then she served the rest of the guests who ate the cake with gusto. Once the cake was eaten, Hannah's father announced that there were presents to open. Filled with excitement, Hannah took off with her cousins and friends into the large front sitting room. The adults took the chairs while the children sat on the floor. A special chair was placed in front of the large picture window for Hannah and one by one, everyone brought her their gifts. There were doll clothes and shoes, piano books, and new ribbons for her hair. Then Grandfather Charles stood up with a small wrapped package in his hand.

"Hannah, my gift is a very special one." He said as he handed it to her, his twinkling blue eyes looking much like her own. Hannah carefully began pulling back the brown paper and blue ribbon, revealing a journal. This was not like any other journal though. This one had a leather cover that was intricately carved with swirling trees, tiny animals, and a beautiful unicorn that graced the center, stealing her gaze from the rest of her gifts. Hannah's eyes softened with pleasure as she traced the carvings with her fingers.

"I made this a long time ago, hoping that someday I would have someone special to give it to. The unicorn on the front is the same one that I talk about in all my stories," Grandfather said.

"Would you tell us a story, Grandfather, about the unicorn?" Hannah pleaded.

"Yes please!" The children agreed as they gathered around Hannah's Grandfather. Grandfather Charles looked at Hannah's father with a question in his eyes.

"Hannah dear, wouldn't you like to go play with your new doll clothes?" Her mother asked.

"No, I want to hear a story. Please Mother please!" Hannah begged.

Her father and mother looked at each other and her father sighed.

"I suppose one story wouldn't hurt," he finally said, running his hand through his hair.

Grandfather Charles smiled at Hannah as he took her place in the chair by the picture window.

"Well now, let's see. What story should I tell?" He placed his hand on his chin, as though he were deep in thought. "I know! I will tell you all the story of the night a unicorn saved me when I was lost in the Dark Woods." He looked around at the wide eyes and eager faces as he started.

"A long time ago, when I was young and strong, I came to Anadulan to seek adventure and riches." As he began, the children all leaned forward and were transported to the depths of the Dark Woods long before any of them were born...

⬗

CHARLES WEAVER HACKED through the dense forest with his machete as he tried to remember which way he had come from. Reluctant to admit he was lost, he kept going, hoping he would find something that he recognized. After going for a few more minutes, he stopped and sighed. Yep, he was lost. Wiping the sweat from his forehead, he scanned his surroundings and strained to see something, anything. He couldn't even see the sun because of the clouds that covered the sky. Maybe he could try to shoot something to eat. After all, he hadn't had anything but dried roots and berries to eat for the past two days, and he was hungry.

Charles sheathed his machete and pulled out his bow from its strap on his back. He strung up the bowstring, loaded an arrow and scanned the woods around him. Walking slowly, Charles backtracked in his path looking for something to shoot at. Spotting a movement to his left, he swung his bow around and aimed. But the creature that he had in his sights stopped him in his tracks. Slowly, he lowered his bow as his eyes widened and his jaw dropped. The beast looked like a regular white horse, but had a single, shimmering white horn coming out of its forehead. Its large, expressive eyes held his gaze as it studied him. As the sun broke through the clouds and shone through the trees, the creature transformed into a misty dream. Its horn caught the light and color flickered and reflected off onto the surrounding leaves. Its long mane hung gently on its silky neck and its eyes shone with life and vibrancy. Charles could not take his eyes off the majestic animal. It moved through the forest away from him with an ethereal beauty and then it disappeared. Scanning the trees wildly, Charles searched for the creature, but couldn't find it. He started off in the direction that it had disappeared, moving as fast as he could through the dense forest. Evening was approaching when he spotted it again. It was watching him with its big eyes, almost humorously. Then it took off again with Charles close behind. As the sun hit the horizon and began to set, the creature disappeared from view and Charles finally realized that he had no idea whatsoever where he was. He had been chasing an unknown being through a dark, dense forest with no sense of direction. For all he knew, he was on the other side of the island, lost forever. For the first time, fear of what might become of him gripped his heart and mind. With no other way to go, he began walking forward again, more slowly this time.

As the sun finally sank below the earth, Charles hit a clearing in the woods and finally realized where he was. Somehow, in chasing the animal through the woods, he had gotten turned around and was heading back to where he started in the first place. The men that had accompanied him to Anadulan were gathered around a fire, eating and laughing loudly at something one of them had said. As Charles strode down the hill into the cleared area, he took one last look at the woods behind him. The creature, magnificent and beautiful, was watching him with its vivid eyes. It shook its mane, nodded its head, and then took off, vanishing into the trees.

Chapter 2

"I will never forget that day," Grandfather Charles said with a faraway look in his eyes. "I found out later that those creatures are known as unicorns. There are many legends about them, but very few people claim to have seen a real one."

The children were enraptured by the story and stared at Grandfather Charles in disbelief.

"Did you ever see it again Grandfather?" Hannah asked.

"Perhaps I have. There have been a few times that I thought I could see it in the woods, but I could never be sure. After that day though, I believed that it watched over me, making sure that I was safe."

The children, with their brilliant imaginations and wide eyes, murmured amongst themselves, debating in their minds whether Grandfather Charles was telling the truth or not. Hannah looked down at the beautiful journal still clutched in her hands. She believed Grandfather Charles, no matter what anyone else said to her. Looking up at him, Hannah said, "Thank you Grandfather. I love my present!" Jumping to her feet, she gave him a big hug. Grandfather chuckled and said, "You're welcome my dear one."

"Alright everyone," Hannah's mother said gently. "It's getting quite late and you children all have school tomorrow."

Reluctantly, Hannah's friends and cousins got up off the floor and went to gather up their things. As Hannah walked out the door of the sitting room, she paused outside the doorway when she heard her father say to Grandfather Charles, "Father, you must stop filling her head with such nonsense. It is not good for Hannah to have her head filled with folly and lore all the time. She needs to stay focused on becoming a lady like her mother so that she can marry well."

"It is not nonsense. I am telling every story exactly like it happened. Hannah should not have to worry about marriage right now. She is barely ten. She should be focused on exploring and creating things."

"I'm telling you right now Father, this must stop. No more stories about unicorns parading about the forest. Have you ever thought about what would happen if she suddenly decided that she wanted to go and find a unicorn? She would get lost in the woods and would possibly never find her way back."

Grandfather didn't respond.

"Besides the point, I am her father and I decide what she should be taught. So, I'm deciding right now that enough is enough. Now that she is ten, she will take lessons daily on becoming a lady and she will stay focused on real life, not fairytales."

Grandfather sighed. "Alright. I won't tell her any more stories, but just remember that she has a vivid imagination. No number of lessons will be able to squelch that."

"I know, but your stories haven't helped that at all."

Their footsteps warned Hannah that her father and Grandfather were approaching the door. Having learned from her mother's stern reprimands that eavesdropping wasn't polite, Hannah bolted down the hallway away from the sitting room door. Her heart sank further with every step. No more stories? Her parents were going to make her take lessons to be a lady? Her favorite parts of the day were the walks that she took with her grandfather through the gardens, letting her imagination run wild.

"Hannah!" Her father called her name. Hannah walked over to the front door where she saw the guests of her party preparing to leave.

"Hannah, would you like to accompany your friends home with your father?" Her mother asked sweetly. Her tone was genuine, but the look that she gave her daughter suggested that Hannah should do it whether she liked to or not because it was the polite thing to do. Hannah wasn't feeling very polite, but she nodded her head and prepared to leave.

After saying goodbye to her aunt, uncle, and cousins, Hannah started down the road with her father, Lottie, and Samantha.

"Do you think that your grandfather's story was true Hannah?" Lottie asked.

"Of course! Grandfather would never lie to us. He tells me all the time that it is important to always tell the truth," Hannah exclaimed, shocked at the fact that Lottie thought Grandfather was making it up.

"But how come no one else has ever seen a unicorn? Don't you think that we would have seen at least one by now?" Samantha asked, the wind blowing wisps of her straight blonde hair across her face.

"Maybe they are really good at hiding," Lottie offered. "I wasn't calling your grandfather a liar Hannah. Don't be upset."

Hannah smiled at her. Lottie never wanted to cause any type of trouble. Contradictory to her vibrant red hair and freckles, she rarely got angry about anything.

They walked in silence for a moment but were soon chatting about Hannah's wonderful party and when they were going to get together again. The walk wasn't a long one, since Lottie and Samantha lived on the same street very close to Hannah's house. On the walk back, Hannah and her father walked in silence for a bit before Hannah asked him, "Why don't you like Grandfather's stories?"

Her father looked up at the sky and sighed softly.

"Hannah, I don't like them because they are not true. There are no such things as unicorns, yet your grandfather continuously insists that they are real. I don't want you to listen to his stories anymore, alright?"

Tears began to form in Hannah's eyes as she looked at the ground, walking in silence. Her father didn't notice that she was crying until they reached the front door of the Weaver house.

"Hannah, what's wrong?" He asked with a gentle voice.

"I love Grandfather's stories, but you aren't going to let him tell them to me anymore, are you?" she said softly, tears pouring down her cheeks.

Her father knelt to her level and used his thumb to wipe the tears from her face before pulling her into his arms. Hannah cried into his shoulder and clung to her father. They stayed there for a moment until he pulled away and looked her in the eyes.

"Hannah, your mother and I want what's best for you. We are not trying to make you upset on purpose, but you are growing up. It's time to focus on becoming a lady, alright? Can you trust us?"

Hannah met his gaze before nodding her head. He gave her one last hug before they went inside the house.

Hannah walked immediately upstairs to her bedroom where her mother had already moved all the presents that she had gotten for her birthday. She spotted the journal that Grandfather Charles had given to her on her desk. Picking it up, Hannah brushed her fingers across the delicate leather cover once again. She did trust her parents, but she still believed that Grandfather's stories were true. Glancing at the cedar chest resting at the foot of her bed, Hannah decided to put the precious journal away until she had a special reason to use it. Walking over to the chest, Hannah opened the lid. Grandfather Charles had made it for her, and when she turned eight, he had shown her the secret compartment he built into the lid. There was a small button near the top of the lid that opened it up. Hannah put her most valued items in there, including her grandmother's pearl necklace in its blue velvet case and the baby blanket that her mother had embroidered for her before she was born. Carefully, Hannah placed the journal inside the lid and closed it again. As far as she knew, only her and Grandfather Charles knew about the secret compartment, so the journal would be safe there.

Suddenly feeling exhausted from her long day preparing for and helping host her party, Hannah took off her beautiful dress and hung it up in her wardrobe before slipping on her nightgown. Outside, she heard rain beginning to hit the roof and the glass windowpane in her room. Once she was in bed, her mother and father came to give her a kiss goodnight and wish her one more happy birthday. Once they were gone, Hannah smiled contentedly. It had been a wonderful birthday, even if she couldn't hear Grandfather's stories anymore. Her eyelids began to get heavy as she slowly drifted off, lulled to sleep by the rhythm of the rain. Unknown to anyone in the household, the side door to the kitchen creaked open, revealing an ill-willing stranger. He silently entered Hannah's home and crept up the stairs to her bedroom. She was so deep in her slumber that she did not hear her door open or the heavy footsteps as the man entered her room. The next thing she knew, she was whipped out of a wonderful dream when he grabbed her roughly out of bed. Before she had a chance to scream, a horrid smelling hand was clamped over her mouth, and a voice that made her heart race and eyes widen whispered in her ear, "Good morning sunshine."

Chapter 3

Her mind racing with fear and terror, Hannah kicked and squirmed as hard as she could to get away from the unseen enemy with an iron grip. But nothing that she did, no matter how hard she fought, could get him to loosen his grip on her. As he carried her through the house to the back door, Hannah became more and more panicked. Tears began to flow from her eyes and she fought harder. Her efforts only caused her kidnapper to slap the side of her head and hiss in her ear,

"Cut it out or I'll hit you so hard that you won't be able to see straight."

His words brought Hannah to a point of despair. If he made it out the back door with her, there was no way that her parents would be able to hear her being taken. As they got closer to the back door, Hannah noticed that the gentle rain that had put her to sleep had turned into an angry thunderstorm, dark and ominous. Getting desperate, Hannah bit her attacker's hand as he reached to open the door.

"Ow!" he exclaimed. "Why you little..."

His grip on her loosened momentarily and Hannah tried to scream, but her voice caught in her throat so that all she could do was squeak before the hand came back over her mouth.

"Now you've done it you little priss."

He slapped her again, harder this time which caused Hannah to cry even more. Once they were out the back door, another man appeared in the rain with two horses. Lightning filled the sky and a rumble of thunder shook the earth.

"What took you so long?" the second man said to the one holding her

"She may be tiny, but she fought me the whole way. She bit me while I was trying to open the door."

The second man looked down at her and grinned evilly.

"She won't have so much fire once she's been tied up in the shack for a few days. Did you leave the note?"

"I didn't dare take my hands off her. You take her. I'll leave the note and I'll meet you at the shack."

"Okay but hurry up. Once the storm lets up, we won't have any cover."

The second man roughly turned Hannah's head to look at him.

"If you try anything, you will regret it. Do you understand me?"

His breath smelled like rotting fish and his eyes gleamed with greed. Hannah swallowed the bile in her throat and nodded her head.

"Good. I'm glad. Now don't scream, or you will make me angry. And when I get angry, people get hurt."

Slowly, the first man lifted his hand off her mouth. Her hands began to tremble, and her vision became blurry as she watched the second man mount up onto his horse. What did they want with her? Why were they taking her? Hannah's head began to spin and her knees gave way, causing her to fall on the ground. The world grew black as she felt herself being lifted by strong arms.

⸻ ❦ ⸻

HANNAH WOKE UP WITH her cheek pressed up against the cold, hard ground. She slowly opened her eyes, groaning at the pain in her head. Where was she? As her vision grew clearer, so did her memory. The hand on her mouth, the rain, the thunder, the pain. She panicked and screamed as loud as she could, frantically trying to loosen the ropes that bound her tightly. She began crying again, trying to figure out what to do. A glance around the dimly lit room that was her prison frightened her even more.

The tiny shack that she was being held in housed floor to ceiling shelves that held a few hunting knives, guns, and food staples like flour and potatoes. Mice scurried across the floor near her feet, startled by her screaming and spider webs filled with flies were the wall's only decor. The only light that she had was coming through the cracks of the ill made walls in front of her. In an attempt to sit up, Hannah realized that she was still in her nightgown, and it was soaked from the rain. Although the weather was warm for springtime, the morning breeze was seeping through the cracks in the walls, causing chills to run up and down her spine. Her muscles ached from the fight that she had put up to avoid being taken and her mouth was dry.

As she began to quiet down, Hannah heard voices on the other side of the wall.

"It's a good thing that we are so far into the woods. That kid can scream."

"You got that right Pete. I'm just glad that she passed out before the ride over here. I'll bet she would've screamed the whole way over. With the fight that she put up in the house, she might've gotten away."

"Yeah. Should we feed her?"

"I don't really want to."

"She is just a kid Joe. It's Steven that we really want to hurt, not her."

"Yeah, but by hurting her, we hurt Steven."

"What if she starves to death before we can get the money from him though. What happens then? Don't you want the money more than revenge?"

"The money is the revenge. I guess we can give her a little bit to eat, but I don't want her to keep up her strength. I want her to be weak and sickly when we give her back."

"Agreed."

There was a shuffling in the room next to her as one of them got up. She heard him rummage through some dishes and then sit back down. Then she smelled it. The food that they were making smelled like bacon and potatoes. Her stomach rumbled and she wondered what time it was. Footsteps sounded in the other room as one of them approached the door. Hannah slunk back into a corner of the tiny shack as the door opened and the one named Pete stepped into the doorway.

"You're lucky my momma raised me with some manners kid. Here. This should keep you from dying."

He placed a bowl with a few pieces of potatoes and bacon in it on the floor near her.

"How am I supposed to eat it with my hands tied?" Hannah whispered, her throat dry.

"Hey Joe," Pete turned into the other room. "We have to untie her if she's gonna eat. Unless you want to hand feed her like a baby."

"Fine, but bring her in here so we can watch her. We've gotten this far. I'd hate for her to escape right before we're rolling in wealth."

Pete grunted his agreement as he turned back to face Hannah.

"Let's go princess," he said as he grabbed her arm in one hand and the bowl in the other. Since her bare feet were still tied, he had to drag her across the floor into the other room. Her freezing feet scraped painfully across the wooden slats in the main room of the shack.

A surprising amount of light was shining into the room and Hannah blinked, catching her first good glimpse of her captors. The one called Joe was tall and lean, and his face was long and weathered. His eyes were a dull green and his hair was a peppered brownish color. He looked and smelled like he hadn't bathed in quite a while. Pete, the one holding her, didn't smell any better. Once he set her on the ground next to the table, he pulled out a knife from his belt and cut the rope binding her hands. Hannah rubbed her sore wrists, trying to regain some feeling in them as she looked up at Pete. Pete looked like he was quite a bit younger than Joe. He had blonde hair similar to hers and golden eyes that showed more life than Joe's, but he still looked mean. If these men had a life quote, it would be 'no mercy'.

Pete placed the bowl in front of her on the floor and said, "Eat. You won't get much else." Hannah didn't need a second invitation. She had to stay strong so that she could escape. The meat was tough and a bit burned, but it still tasted pretty good. Joe put a cup of water next to her bowl. Hannah grabbed it and downed it in two gulps. The water was cold and felt good going down her parched throat. The fire in the main room was beginning to warm her freezing body and she felt a little bit better with food in her belly. Once she was finished eating though, Pete tied her back up and dragged her across the floor to the lean-to. Once she was inside, he pulled the door shut and she heard his heavy footsteps going back across the wooden floor to the table.

Hannah looked around the lean-to again and began to think of ways that she could escape. There were two knives on shelves on the wall opposite of her. One was up on a higher shelf, but the other was closer to the floor. If she could stand up, maybe she could reach it. Suddenly filled with determination, Hannah attempted to get her legs beneath her body. It was harder than she thought. She tried sitting up really fast, but she couldn't keep her balance. Then she tried rolling over on her side, but she could only get to her knees. After trying for what seemed like eternity, Hannah laid still. She was panting and tired from her efforts. Without even trying, she fell asleep on the floor.

When Hannah woke up again, the lean-to was darkening. It must've been almost nighttime. Shaking the sleepiness out of her head, she tried another time to stand up. This time, after making it to her knees, she put her head on the ground and pushed as hard as she could. To her surprise, she made it! Now if only she could grab the knife. Hannah carefully hopped to the opposite wall hoping to reach the lower shelf, but it was still too high. Tears pricked her eyes as she began to give up hope.

The last rays of sunshine were leaving the cracks of her walled prison when one of them hit a gleaming object hiding under the bottom shelf. Hannah hopped back over to the shelf and fell to her knees to see what it was. She peered into the darkness under the wood shelf and almost gasped in delight. It was an old axe head, broken but still useful.

Footsteps approaching caused her to roll away from it and lie still with her back to the door. When it opened, she heard Pete say sarcastically,

"We have your dinner ready for you 'your highness.'"

His strong hand grabbed her arm and, once again, she was dragged across the floor into the main room of the shack. Dinner was ham and potatoes and one cup of water. She ate and drank without a word. Her mind was on her escape plan. Once her captors went to bed, she would sneak out. She had been listening to see if any of the boards on the floor squeaked so she could avoid them. All she had to do was pray that neither of them stood watch for the night. After dinner, Hannah was dragged back into her prison for the night. There, she waited patiently for the opportune moment to escape.

Chapter 4

The minutes ticked by slowly as Hannah waited for Pete and Joe to go to bed. She listened to them talk about their weapons and her, but then she heard her father's name again.

"Did we demand enough money from Steven, do you think?" Pete asked.

"I think so. It should set him back for months. He'll pay for what he did to us," Joe replied.

Hannah's curiosity peaked as she listened to their conversation. What were they talking about?

"Are you sure that he's going to pay that much?" Pete asked again.

"Of course! We have his daughter, his only child! He would pay anything to get her back."

"You're probably right. We're sure she can't get out right?"

"She's ten years old. What is she going to do, scream until the windows crack?"

"Maybe. Didn't you leave your hunting knives in there?"

"Yeah, but she's not tall enough to reach them."

"You're sure?"

"Would you stop worrying! She's not going to escape! Unless you didn't tie her up tight enough." Joe challenged.

"Hey, don't question my knots! That was one thing that I was good at until YOU got us fired. Remember, stealing Steven's money was your idea."

"Give me a break, you went right along with it. I didn't have to ask you twice. You were in as soon as you heard money was involved."

"Yeah, but I wasn't the one who kept wanting more. I was content to just take a little bit at a time, but NO. You HAD to keep getting more and more."

"Don't question my leadership! Who gave up the whole story once Steven started suspecting us?"

"I did it hoping that he would blame you and not me!"

"Why you no good, dirty rotten pig. You're lucky that you know too much about this gig or I would've thrown you out already."

"You couldn't have done it without me and you know it."

"Whatever you say kid," Joe said with a condescending tone.

Pete huffed and said, "I'm going to hit the hay. Make sure that you check up on the girl before you go to bed."

"Yeah, whatever," Joe replied.

Pete grumbled under his breath as Hannah heard him get up from his chair and stalk across the room. She heard shoes drop onto the wood floor and one of the beds creak as he laid down. Now she was listening even more closely to hear when Joe got up. He seemed content to sit there forever. Hannah found herself fighting to stay awake waiting for him to move.

Just as she was starting to doze off, she heard a chair scrape across the floor and footsteps approach the door. When the door opened, she shut her eyes and pretended to be asleep so that he wouldn't suspect anything. Once he closed the door, Joe walked immediately to bed and dropped his shoes onto the floor like Pete had done. The bed creaked as Joe laid down atop it. Within moments, Hannah heard him snoring loudly. That was her cue to jump into action. She scooted her body over to the shelf, feeling her way around in the dark until she reached it.

The next part would be challenging. Somehow, Hannah had to sit up but still be able to reach underneath the shelf to cut the ropes on her hands. Pulling herself up, Hannah bent her elbows towards her front and began to search for the axe head. The sharp metal pricked her finger when she found it, but she barely felt a thing, the prospect of escaping pumping adrenaline through her veins. Slowly but surely, Hannah moved her wrists back and forth on the sharp axe head until she felt the rope begin to give way under the pressure.

With one final push, the rope that bound her hands broke. She was free! Now for her feet. Feeling in the darkness for the course rope, Hannah found that the knot was loose enough to be untied. Once her feet were free, Hannah stood up and began feeling along the wall for the door that would let her out into the open. Staying quiet was a crucial part of her plan. If either of the men sleeping in the next room found out that she was escaping, there was no telling what they might do to her.

Finding the door, Hannah lifted the latch and slowly opened it, grimacing when it squeaked a little bit. The dying fire in the hearth gave off a small fragment of light, allowing her to see where she was going. Tip toeing gently across the wooden slats on the floor, Hannah made her way over to the door that led outside. Taking one last look behind her to make sure that both men were still asleep, Hannah breathed deeply and twisted the doorknob. It opened without any trouble, so she slipped outside. After shutting it softly behind her, Hannah pressed her ear to the door, straining to hear if her captors had stirred.

Hearing nothing, she ran into the woods. Her only light being the nearly full moon, she ran into the night, dodging trees and shrubs. Vines brushed up against her face and thorns dug themselves into the skin of her bare arms and legs. Hannah didn't know where she was running to, but she didn't care. She just wanted to be free of those horrid men. Hannah only stopped running when she couldn't breathe. Leaning up against a tree, she huffed and wheezed. Her legs were quivering and sweat dripped from her forehead despite the cool breeze that blew her white-blonde hair around her face.

Hannah looked around her and for the first time was afraid of the woods. When she was in the shack, they seemed like a safe haven, but now they just looked scary. The moon that had lit her way to freedom now cast shadows that moved when she wasn't looking. The wind that had pushed her to run faster now made eerie sounds that filled her ears. Hannah's imagination was running wild with all the possible terror that awaited her in the Dark Woods at night.

Hearing a branch break on her left side, Hannah swung around, straining to see through the dimly lit foliage. She thought that she saw a shadow move through the trees and her heart dropped into her stomach. Was some unseen animal lurking in the dark waiting to eat her? Slowly, Hannah sank to the ground, still leaning up against the tree. She wrapped her arms around her knees and drew them close to her chest. Not wanting to see any more moving shadows or unblinking eyes in the dark, she placed her head down on her knees and began to cry. She missed her mother and father.

She hadn't even thought of her parents until now. What were they thinking? Surely, they were trying to find her, but how would they find her in the Dark Woods? Thinking about her parents made her cry even harder. Would she ever see them again? Was she going to die in these woods? Tears falling onto her soiled nightgown, Hannah cried herself to sleep without taking any notice to the big eyes carefully watching her through the leaves.

Chapter 5

A sharp crack woke Hannah up. Sitting up board straight, she didn't dare move. The crack had sounded like a gunshot. What if Pete and Joe found out she was gone? Her suspicions were proven correct when she heard voices echoing through the quiet woods, getting closer every second. Hannah's heart beat wildly as she looked around for a hiding place. Spotting a group of flowering bushes, she crawled as quickly as she could to them and settled herself in their depths. Her nightgown, thoroughly soiled, acted as a sort of camouflage, so she had no trouble blending in with the night.

Hannah wrapped her arms around her knees again and prayed that she wouldn't be seen. A yellow light appeared, growing brighter as the men drew closer. They were arguing with each other.

"I told you we should have checked the room. You didn't even see the axe head under the shelf. This is your fault!" Pete's voice cut through the night.

"Don't blame this on me. If we hadn't fed her, maybe she would be too weak to break free. Now whose idea was that? Oh yeah, yours!"

"Oh please. You have a heart so cold that you could slap a baby and not feel any remorse. At least I was raised decently."

"Just be quiet so we can listen for her. She couldn't have gotten far. It's so dark in these woods that you can barely see anything."

Their footsteps drew closer and closer until they were almost upon her. Hannah held her breath as they stopped right next to her hiding spot. The torch's light almost touched the tips of her toes, but she drew them back further to avoid being seen. A twig snapped to her left on the other side of the flowering bushes she was hiding in. Pete and

Joe swung around and raced after the sound. More twigs snapped and leaves rustled as something fled from her captors.

Once they were gone, Hannah jumped from her hiding spot and raced in the opposite direction they were going. Her breath came in short gasps as she pushed herself faster and faster. The further she got away from those men, the safer she felt. Her head started spinning from lack of oxygen and she was forced to stop. Falling on her knees, Hannah sucked in big gulps of air, her legs unable to carry her any further.

Spotting an outcropping of rocks surrounded by massive pine trees, she pulled her tired body into its shelter and curled up in a ball on the mossy ground. The stars overhead shone over top of her, as if reassuring her that they were watching out for her. Thinking about her parents again, Hannah began to cry softly, the warm tears a sharp contrast to her cold, wind whipped cheeks. She thought about her Grandfather Charles and how worried he must be. Would he come looking for her? If anyone knew the Dark Woods, it would be Grandfather. After all, he had been an explorer. As exhaustion took over, Hannah's eyes drifted shut and she fell into a deep sleep.

While Hannah slept, a large creature began to creep towards her, moving silently through the trees. Its body reflected the white light of the moon and its graceful footfalls mere whispers on the mossy forest floor. Curious of the crying little girl, the animal studied her with its large, gentle eyes. When it drew close enough to reach her, the creature sniffed Hannah's hair and nuzzled her face. When Hannah didn't respond, the beast laid down beside her, snuggling close to Hannah's small, shivering body, keeping her warm and watching the woods for any predator that would dare show itself.

———— ◉ ————

HANNAH AND GRANDFATHER Charles were walking hand in hand in the Dark Woods. The sunlight spilling from the treetops gave the forest a mystical glow. Hannah held Grandfather's hand tightly as she scanned the forest, looking for anything. Her beautiful white party dress swished around her ankles, brushing gently against the leaves of the bushes that they passed.

"Hannah, unicorns are real," Grandfather Charles said. "Today, you will see for yourself what they look like."

"I believe you Grandfather!" Hannah replied. "Where are they?"

"They are coming. They are coming for you."

Hannah turned to her Grandfather with a surprised look in her eyes. "Why are they coming for me?" she asked.

"For the same reason they came for me. You are in trouble," Grandfather said simply.

"How am I in trouble Grandfather? You are here with me."

"Yes, but not for too much longer."

"Are you going to leave me?" Hannah asked, surprised at him. Grandfather would never leave her. Would he?

"It's not my choice to leave, dear. I would stay if I could, but I can't."

"What am I going to do?" Hannah asked as she looked around the woods. "I don't remember which way to go."

"They will find you Hannah. Don't be afraid."

Hannah turned to look at him, but he was gone. She spun around wildly in a circle looking for him. Where could he have gone?

"Grandfather!" Hannah yelled into the forest. Hannah began running back the way that she thought they had come, but somehow, she was getting all turned around in different directions.

"Grandfather!" She yelled out again. The forest seemed to close in around her. She couldn't find her way.

The lovely rays of yellow sunshine that had been streaming through the trees turned so dark that Hannah could barely see where she was going. The bushes that had been gently brushing her skirt turned into thorns that tore her pretty dress. Rocks appeared in her way and Hannah tripped, falling into the dirt. Standing up again, she saw her white dress covered in dust, dried leaves, and grass.

Tears started to spill from her eyes as she cried out, "Grandfather! Where are you!"

To her left, she heard her grandfather's voice say, "They are coming Hannah. Don't be afraid."

Hannah spun around to see where the voice had come from, but didn't find anyone there. Suddenly, in the still night, she heard footsteps approaching. Hannah's eyes widened with fear and she began to whimper, "Please. Please don't hurt me."

The bushes in front of her began to rustle. Something was moving in them. Hannah squinted her eyes, straining to see what was there. Then, right before her eyes, the most beautiful creature she had ever seen appeared. The moon shone off its body and the stars were in its eyes. Its long mane and tail nearly brushed the ground, hanging in silky strands. From its forehead, a single horn twinkled and shimmered from the light in the sky. It looked at her with gentle eyes and Hannah knew immediately what it was. It looked exactly like the carving on the journal that Grandfather Charles had given to her on her birthday. It was a unicorn. Grandfather was right. They were real!

As Hannah reached out to touch it, she heard voices coming from the bushes to her right. To her horror, Joe and Pete emerged, enraged at her escape. When they saw the unicorn though, both raised up their guns to shoot it. Hannah screamed and lunged forward to block their bullets, but she was too late. The beautiful unicorn was dead and she would be next. Looking at the two men, Hannah couldn't move. Some unseen force was holding her back as they got closer and closer. She tried to scream, but no sound came out of her mouth. She tried to swing her fists and kick her legs, but she couldn't move. Terror gripped her heart as they grabbed her once again...

❦

WITH A GASP, HANNAH woke up. She was still laying under the same trees that she had fallen asleep under earlier after running from

Pete and Joe. The darkness was overwhelming her, causing her to imagine sounds and deadly voices. Noticing that the rocks behind her were not cold anymore, Hannah reached out her hand and felt a warm body with her fingers. Fear shook her to the core until a gentle sound emerged from the darkness, urging her closer. Her mind not even registering what it might be, she snuggled up against the protective warmth and closed her eyes again, praying that she wouldn't have another nightmare. As Hannah drew closer, the steady rhythm of a heartbeat sounded in her ears and lulled her back into sweet and restful sleep.

Chapter 6

Hannah was awakened the next morning to birds singing and warm sunlight shining on her. She opened her eyes slowly, trying to make the drowsiness go away. Sitting up, Hannah turned to look at the thing that had kept her warm all night. Her eyes widened and she leapt backward, not believing what she saw. The beautiful creature stood to its feet and watched her with gentle eyes. Its silky mane and tail hung down almost to the ground and its body caught the sun's rays, making it look like a dream. One single horn was protruding from its forehead, shimmering a million colors in the new light. It was a unicorn. A unicorn had found her in the night and had kept her from freezing to death.

Unable to react in any way, Hannah just stood there, jaw dropped and eyes wide, waiting to see what it would do. The unicorn seemed content where it was, watching her with its big brown eyes. They both just stood there for a while, studying each other. Hannah was still in disbelief. So all of Grandfather's stories were true? He hadn't made any of them up? There had always been a part of her that wondered if his stories were exaggerated or made up, but the unicorn looked exactly like the one that he had described to her in his story about being lost in the woods.

Suddenly being overcome by desire, Hannah stretched out her hand to the unicorn, hoping that she might be able to touch it. She kept reminding herself that this was a wild animal and could stomp on her any time it wanted, but looking in the unicorn's eyes, Hannah couldn't believe that it would do anything to hurt her. As she stretched her hand out, the unicorn reached its muzzle out to meet it. The moment that they touched, a connection sprang to life and Hannah no longer felt afraid. She felt as though she were on top of the whole world and nothing could defeat her.

Her heart began to race as she stared into the unicorn's eyes. Hannah smiled and giggled, surprised at the joy and vibrancy that was rushing through her body. The unicorn nickered and playfully tossed its head, nibbling on Hannah's hair. The action made Hannah giggle even more and she threw her arms around its neck, burying her face into its long silky mane.

A gasp behind her caused Hannah's heart to drop and she spun around, afraid of who was there. But it wasn't Pete or Joe watching her. It was a man unlike anyone she had ever seen before. He didn't dress like the people she met in town. He wore brown leggings and a long brown tunic. His shoes didn't have buckles on them, rather they had laces and he wore odd looking jewelry. His hair was long and dark, almost to his waist, and one of his ears was pierced with a single gold hoop. He was staring at her and the unicorn with amazement in his deep hazel eyes. Hannah hid behind the unicorn's beautiful neck and watched him closely.

When he motioned for her to come near, Hannah shook her head and took a step back. He tried to speak to her, but he didn't speak any language that she knew, so she shook her head again. He held up one finger, telling her to wait and disappeared from the pine grove. When he came back, he had something in his hand that looked like a piece of bacon and Hannah's stomach growled. He sat down right at the edge of the grove and smiled at her. Then he ripped the meat into two pieces and tossed one half in her direction, putting the other half in his mouth showing her that it was good to eat.

Hannah moved forward to grab the food and hurried back to the safety of the unicorn. She put the piece of meat in her mouth and took a bite. It was tough and hard, but it tasted good, and she was hungry enough that she didn't care too much. Within moments, the meat was gone. The man motioned to himself and said, "Noo-ashi."

Hannah, confused, said, "What?"

"Noo-ashi," he repeated, gesturing to himself again.

Hannah pointed at him and repeated what he had said, "Noo-ashi?"

He smiled and nodded as he replied one more time, "Noo-ashi."

Then Hannah understood. Noo-ashi must be his name. When he pointed at her, she said, "Hannah."

"Hannah," he repeated. He smiled at her as he motioned once again for her to come and pointed to the unicorn. Hannah looked at the animal and decided that Noo-ashi meant for the unicorn to go with her. She grabbed a fistful of its mane and began to walk slowly forward. The unicorn followed without complaint.

Noo-ashi didn't touch her or try to grab her. He just walked in front of her, looking back occasionally, to make sure that she was still following him. Eventually, they came to a giant waterfall that spilled into a rushing river. To her surprise, Noo-ashi walked right up to the waterfall along a slab of rock that served as a pathway. Then he disappeared behind the roaring water. Hannah hesitated, but eventually followed him, the unicorn still next to her, unafraid. She expected to be drenched, but the path had led behind the waterfall to a cavern, not underneath it.

Noo-ashi was waiting for her when she emerged and motioned for her to follow him again. Hannah nodded and walked forward, still clinging to the unicorn's mane. It was dark in the cavern, but there was light coming from somewhere. Then she realized that the cave was actually a tunnel that led to the other side of the river. When they reached the end of the tunnel, more woods stretched out before them, but Noo-ashi seemed to know where he was going, which comforted Hannah.

The walk seemed to never end and Hannah was growing tired again. She spoke up and said Noo-ashi's name. He turned to her and Hannah tried to let him know she needed a break by rubbing her bare feet. He nodded and began to walk towards her. Hannah began to cower, afraid that he might try to carry her. Instead though, he lifted her up and placed her on the back of the unicorn. Surprised at both his reaction and the unicorn's lack of one, Hannah let out a little gasp. Noo-ashi looked at her face, making sure she was okay, before he started walking again. Without any command, the unicorn began to follow him, so Hannah took two big fistfuls of its mane so as not to fall off.

Now Hannah was thoroughly confused. She had watched stable hands break in wild horses before and none of the beasts had broken willingly. In fact, many of the horses had ended up hurting the stable hand trying to train them. Why didn't the unicorn do anything about her on its back? Was it already trained? If so, who trained it? Did they know that their unicorn was missing? All of her questions faded as the revelation of her situation started to sink in. She was riding on a unicorn just like a princess in one of her fairy tale stories. Although she was pretty sure she didn't look like a princess. She was still wearing her white nightgown. At least it used to be white. It was now covered in dirt, muddy tears, and grass stains. It would be fair to say that the gown would never come clean.

As their journey went on, Hannah marveled at the little creatures that scurried through the woods all around her, unafraid of the unicorn she was riding on. In fact, at one point, two birds had landed on its mane right in front of her. They peeked at her with their little beady eyes before flying away again. The sunshine was warm on her back and a slight breeze blew her long hair away from her face. The unicorn's muscles moved rhythmically beneath Hannah's bare legs and the air smelled like sun and rain mixed with the subtle scent of new flowers and warm dirt.

Still following Noo-ashi, Hannah and the unicorn crossed a small stream and climbed up a hill. Noo-ashi beat her there and stood tall, waiting for her with a smile on his face. As Hannah crested the hill, she looked down and saw a darling little village, filled with tiny huts and tents. Children were running around, laughing and playing with their mothers looking on. There was one large fire in the middle of the camp that the men were using to cook a meal. The most wonderful smells came wafting up and reached Hannah's nose, causing her stomach to rumble again. The village was in the center of a small clearing at the bottom of the hill, so Noo-ashi began walking again with Hannah close behind him.

When the people of the tiny village saw Noo-ashi, they smiled, but when they saw Hannah and the unicorn, their jaws dropped. The closer they came to the village, the more people appeared, all of them in awe of the scene that stood before them. As Noo-ashi led her straight down the middle of the village, Hannah noticed that all the people around her had begun to bow as she passed. Confused, Hannah wondered who they thought she was.

When Hannah had reached the central fire, Noo-ashi lifted his hands up to her, ready to let her down. Hannah didn't want to get down, but her curiosity got the best of her. She let Noo-ashi take her down from the unicorn and looked at the people around her. They were watching her and the unicorn intently, with big wondrous eyes. Finally, an older man stepped forward and began to speak to her in a language that she didn't know. Hannah shook her head and shrugged her shoulders. Then she pointed to her ears, trying to communicate that she didn't know what he was saying. The older man seemed to understand and began to speak to Noo-ashi. Noo-ashi nodded at his words and ran off into the midst of the huts. Although Hannah didn't really know him, she was sad when he left. She clung to the unicorn's mane, then turned to face it. It was watching her with its beautiful eyes, unafraid of their situation. Its courage gave Hannah some amount of bravery.

Hannah turned back to the older man and told him her name like Noo-ashi had done back in the pine grove.

"Hannah," she said, gesturing to herself. Then she pointed at him.

The old man smiled at her and replied, "Li-kani." Then he said, "Vespen Hannah," motioning to the crowd around her. In one voice, they called out, "Vespen Hannah!"

Hannah figured it was some sort of welcoming term, but she didn't know for sure. Motioning again to the crowd, Li-kani said, "Sephramin."

"What?" Hannah said.

Li-kani began to walk among the people saying, "Sephramin. Sephramin. Sephramin."

He began pointing to the huts and the fires while saying the same word, "Sephramin. Sephramin. Sephramin."

Hannah was beginning to understand. The tribe's name must be Sephramin. Hannah pointed to a little girl standing in front of her.

"Sephramin?" she asked. The little girl blushed and rushed to hide behind her mother's legs.

Li-kani nodded. "Yah," he said. "Sephramin."

Hannah smiled at all of the people around her and repeated the name one last time, "Sephramin." The people were all smiling and nodding at her.

Then Noo-ashi appeared again. He was leading a very old woman by the hand through the crowd who appeared to be blind. She was calling out, "Who? Who? Who is here?"

"Hannah," Noo-ashi told her. He motioned for Hannah to draw close. Slowly, Hannah began walking towards her as the woman reached out her hands. When Hannah was close enough, Noo-ashi put the woman's hands on Hannah's face. The woman began to move her hands over Hannah's face as if trying to envision what she looked like and then smiled.

"Hannah, I am Soo-shani. The Sephramin welcome you to our home. You, my child, have been chosen by a white star. Once chosen by a unicorn, you are chosen forever."

Chapter 7

"You know English?" Hannah asked the woman.

"Yes my dear, I do. I was not born into the Sephramin tribe, I married a Sephramin man. My family died when I was young, so I found refuge in the trees of this forest. My husband, Soo-ashi, died many years ago, but I have found my place here with these people."

Hannah's fear was lessened when she heard Soo-shani's story. It was comforting to know that someone spoke her language.

"Our leader, Chief Li-kani, would like to speak with you," Soo-Shani said to Hannah. Hannah swallowed hard and walked with the woman over to Chief Li-kani. As the chief spoke, Soo-shani translated for Hannah.

"We welcome you to our home, chosen one of the stars. We are ready to provide whatever you may need," Soo-shani translated.

"What do you mean 'chosen one of the stars'? I haven't been chosen by a star. I don't even know what you are talking about."

"Our people have many legends about the creatures called unicorns. It is said that they are stars that fell from the heavens. They walk about the earth looking for someone who is worthy of their friendship. Once they have chosen someone, they have chosen forever. Even when they pass and return once more to the sky, they still watch over their chosen one. Their horn is a part of their star form, reminding us who they are. They look forward to the day that they are reunited with their brothers and sisters in the sky, racing with the sun and dancing with the moon."

Hannah didn't know what to say to that. Grandfather had told her about unicorns, but never had she heard such a story. It would explain why the unicorn's horn shimmered in the sunlight, its rays bringing out the thousands of colors were hidden within it.

"What have you named her?"

"It's a girl?"

"Yes, it is."

"I didn't name her anything yet. What would a good name be for a unicorn?"

Chief Li-kani thought for a moment before replying, "A unicorn should be named something majestic and powerful."

"What about Moonlight?"

Soo-shani nodded at Hannah and replied, "In our language, Moonlight is Luna-min."

"I like that name. I could call her Luna for short!"

Hannah turned to the unicorn and said, "Do you like your new name Luna?"

Luna shook her head up and down, causing her silky mane to be tossed in the wind. Hannah smiled at her. Chief Li-kani motioned to Hannah and Soo-shani translated again.

"How did you come to be lost in the forest? You are a long way from the sea port."

Hannah shuddered as she recounted the night before.

"I was asleep in my room when two horrible men snatched me away and took me to a shack in the woods. I managed to escape them by running into the forest, but I got lost trying to get away."

Soo-shani translated to the chief and a look of horror passed across his face. He spoke again to Soo-shani with angry words. Hannah cowered back into Luna as she listened to him speak. Noo-ashi took notice of her fear and spoke calmly to the chief, gesturing to Hannah. The chief looked at Hannah and held his hands up as if he were trying to show her he meant no harm and spoke again. Hannah looked at Soo-shani, her heart pounding in her ears.

"Chief Li-kani is angry that those men did that to you. He says that we will take you back to your home tomorrow."

Hannah nodded slowly and said softly, "Thank you."

The chief spoke again to Soo-shani who then spoke to Hannah.

"You are in need of food and clothing. If you go with these women and myself, we will help you get cleaned up and dressed."

Three women stepped forward with smiles on their faces and motioned for Hannah to follow them, one of them leading Soo-shani. As Hannah walked after them, Luna followed close behind Hannah, never leaving her for a moment. Hannah reached out for Luna and clung to her mane again. The Sephramins were nice, but she was still a little bit scared. What if they decided they didn't want to bring her back? What if Pete and Joe found her again in the night when everyone was sleeping? Looking down at her ruined nightgown and feeling the hunger in her stomach, Hannah's mind shifted off her fears and onto the Sephramin's offering. At least she would be able to eat and change. She scanned the hill where she and Noo-ashi had climbed down minutes ago and noticed a group of men spread out over the top, their bows ready to defend at any sign of danger. That made Hannah feel much safer.

The women and Soo-shani led Hannah to a river near the back of the clearing. There, they helped her wash off the dirt and grime that covered her body and clear her long blonde hair of the leaves and twigs that had tangled themselves up. When she was clean, another woman appeared with some clothing for her. When Hannah saw what they were dressing her in, she was pleasantly surprised. All of it was white doeskin, cured so that it was soft to the touch. There were leggings that came down to her ankles and a short sleeved tunic that fell just above her knees. The woman that called herself Loo-kani helped her lace up the bead encrusted doeskin shoes, their softness soothing her aching feet.

Taking out a sort of comb, Loo-kani slowly worked her way through Hannah's thick blonde hair, murmuring something to the other women. Curious, Hannah asked Soo-shani, "What is she saying?"

Soo-shani smiled and said, "She is saying that you have the hair of an angel. She is trying to decide if Luna chose you because you are a lost star like her."

Hannah's heart warmed at Soo-shani's anwer and waited patiently until Loo-kani was done.

When Loo-kani had finished combing Hannah's hair, she began to braid it down her back, tying it off with a leather strap. Tiny ringlets began to fall from the braid and curl around Hannah's face, making her look more and more angelic. The women smiled and spoke in their language to each other as they admired their handiwork. As Soo-shani translated, Hannah learned that Loo-kani wasn't the only one who thought that she was beautiful like an angel. All the women who were helping her believed that she was some sort of heavenly being.

The entire time that Hannah was getting ready, Luna had stood patiently, grazing on the luscious green grass that covered the valley. Now that she was ready, Hannah approached her. Luna looked up at her and shook her head, meeting Hannah's blue eyes with her deep brown ones. Hannah wrapped her arms around Luna's neck and stood there for a moment. When she let go and turned around, she saw that the women had been watching her, awestruck at the bond that had so quickly formed between "the Angel" and "the Star". Hannah blushed and cast her eyes down to the ground.

The group of women laughed at her shyness and took her by the hand, leading her back to the camp where delicious smells had begun to fill the air. Hannah's stomach began to complain loudly as they made their way through the camp to the big fire in the center. Her eyes widened as she noticed the huge boar on a spit, spinning slowly over the roaring blaze. Blankets had been laid out over a section of the ground and were covered with clay and wooden bowls. The bowls held berries, grains, roots, and water.

As she took in the scene, Hannah noticed that Noo-ashi was the one slowly turning the spit over the fire. When she caught his eye, she smiled at him, causing his tanned face to morph into a huge grin. He announced something in his native tongue and everyone turned to look at her. As she walked through the crowd of people, they smiled at her, some of them even patting her shoulder or head as she passed. The women that had helped her get ready led her to Chief Li-kani, who welcomed her with a smile and a nod. Loo-kani walked right up to the chief and kissed his cheek before saying something to him. Hannah turned to Soo-shani and asked with a confused look on her face, "Are Chief Li-kani and Loo-kani married?"

Soo-shani chuckled at her question and replied, "No. Loo-kani is Chief Li-kani's daughter. His wife died three years ago while giving birth to a son. Neither mother nor son made it."

Hannah nodded her head and turned back to face the chief, who was looking at her intently. His staring was starting to make Hannah feel uncomfortable until he began speaking. As Soo-shani translated, Hannah's eyes widened with shock and wonder.

"We believe that you were chosen by Luna-min because you are her sister from the stars. Moonlight shines from your hair and your eyes are filled with the clear morning sky. Now we offer you whatever you need to continue on your journey." Chief Li-kani finished and gestured to the crowd of natives behind him who had not stopped staring in awe at Hannah.

As if on cue, Luna, standing next to Hannah, nodded her head and let out a loud whinny. Hannah giggled and put her arms around Luna, peeking at the Chief through her long mane. With her stomach still grumbling, Hannah asked, "Could we maybe eat something now?" After Soo-shani translated, Chief Li-kani laughed and motioned her forward. Noo-ashi handed her a wooden bowl and cut off a piece of the delicious smelling boar for her. A woman sitting on the blankets served her berries, nuts, and a scoop of odd looking mush, but Hanah took it without complaint. She was so hungry that she might've eaten the boar raw.

Once she had her food, Soo-Shani called for Hannah to go sit by her. Everyone around her had begun to get their share of the food and were starting to eat. Sitting down next to Soo-shani, Hannah gingerly picked up the piece of meat and carefully bit off a chunk. It tasted like smoke and was a little bit chewy, but it was good. Not even thinking about her manners, Hannah scarfed down the rest of the meat along with the nuts and berries. The mush tasted like bread in an odd sort of way and soon that was gone too.

"Soo-shani. Is there more?" Hannah asked tentatively.

Soo-shani chuckled at Hannah and said, "Go on and ask. There is more than enough for everyone."

Hannah didn't need a second invitation. She didn't waste any time making her way back toward the fire pit. Noo-ashi smiled at her and said something in his native tongue. Hannah tilted her head with a confused look on her face. He laughed at her and pointed to his belly repeating what he said. Hannah still didn't quite understand, but she assumed he was referring to her still being hungry, so she smiled back and nodded quickly.

Noo-ashi laughed again and began cutting off another piece of the roasted boar, this time giving her a bit of a bigger chunk. Hannah thanked him and walked back over to Soo-shani, smiling at the children that kept reaching out, trying to touch her hair. Even the boys and girls around her age were peering at her through the fingers that covered their eyes, their mouths curved up in shy smiles. Soo-shani heard her coming and said,

"The children have never seen someone with light hair and blue eyes. Not even I, being an outsider, looked like you do."

"How did they find you Soo-shani?" Hannah asked innocently.

Soo-shani's eyes softened with pleasure as she recounted the beloved story.

Chapter 8

"I was young when my parents died, only 11 years old. They were the only family that I had on this island and we were very poor, so our house was on the outskirts of town. None of the rich merchants wanted to see us because we were not people of status, so we lived all on our own. My mother was with child when my father became ill. The day after he died, my mother went into labor, but neither she, nor the baby survived. I didn't know what to do. I was not able to go to school, so I didn't have any friends. There was no one that I could turn to, so I fled into the woods."

"But the woods are so scary!" Hannah exclaimed.

"Maybe to you dear one, but not to me. I had grown up in them. I knew what sort of creatures lived where and what plants were good to eat. I had been wandering for almost two days when a young man, slightly older than me, found me in the woods. He wanted me to go with him, but I didn't know where he would take me, so I refused. He left me for a time, but came back not too much later with a woman who looked about the age of my mother. I found out later that she was his mother and that his name was Soo-ashi. They took me in and cared for me. I was able to communicate to them through a sort of sign language that my parents were both dead. The Sephramin take death very seriously, so they helped me bury my parents and baby brother. After that, I decided to stay with them."

"You didn't want to live in town?" Hannah asked, completely in awe of Soo-shani's story.

"No. The people there didn't treat me with respect because I wasn't like any of them. I considered going back for a little while, but I found my place with the Sephramin. They are my people and I belong with them. My husband died a few years ago, but he was the one who found me in the woods. His family became my family, and his friends became my friends. He taught me the Sephramin language and how to live like his people. My heart is here and will never leave this beautiful place." Soo-shani finished, her eyes, though blinded, looking off into the distance as she recounted her life.

Hannah watched her thoughtfully and then looked in the direction that she was looking. The sun was beginning to set and the fiery orange and red colors shone down onto the valley, bathing the grass in the purest of light. As the sun sank below the horizon, the vibrant orange and red faded into a wispy pink and yellow. Looking up, Hannah saw a single star shine down on her from up above. She could understand why Soo-shani didn't ever want to leave. It was beautiful here and there didn't seem to be a care in the world.

The gentle sounds of a whispered melody reached her ears and Hannah turned around just as a drum began to play. A young man and woman stood on the hill behind her with a drum and a flute, entertaining the younger children. The older adults had begun to dance with each other around the fire, laughing and singing in their foreign tongue. Noo-ashi walked over to Hannah and held out his hand, silently asking her if she would like to dance. Hannah giggled and placed her hand in his.

The dance wasn't like any dance that Hannah had seen before. It did not have strict moves to follow and it wasn't dark and brooding. The dance had a light-heartedness that caused a joyous feeling to rise in her heart. Noo-ashi swung her around the fire and began to sing with his people. Though Hannah didn't know the words, she did her best to sing the melody, not wanting to be left out. She had never felt so happy in all her life. Luna was still there next to Soo-shani, watching her carefully, the children were dancing in little circles and clapping, and her new friends were singing and dancing with her.

When the song was over, Hannah curtsied to Noo-ashi and skipped back over to Soo-shani and Luna. Chief Li-kani followed her to Soo-shani and asked the older woman something. Soo-shani seemed reluctant to answer, but finally smiled and nodded her head.

"What did he ask?" Hannah inquired.

"He asked me if I would sing a song for them. The children like to hear it," Soo-shani replied.

As the little children began to gather around Soo-shani's feet, their expectations high, the whole valley came to a hush. Soo-shani took a breath and began to sing with a quiet, lilting tone, a song that had been long forgotten by the world.

———◉———

"Long were the days when earth and sky were one.
Man stood together blessed by the sun.
Stars shone from heaven, smiling at the moon.
No one could imagine what was coming soon.
Man fell into what we know as sin.
No one loved his brother to the end.
Man's noble Maker watched in disbelief.
How could all this happen? All they knew was grief.
Then fell from heaven creatures of the stars,
choosing to walk with man despite his scars.
Pure, noble, honest men these creatures made.
Sent by their Creator, there on earth they stayed
Soon days will come when those who live in fear
Stand up and cry out, "Maker draw me near!"
When that day comes the stars that He sent down,
He'll call back to the heavens and come to earth Himself.

AS SOO-SHANI'S SONG faded into the night, the rustling of the trees and the cricket's chirping softened the silence. The adults began to murmur amongst themselves, quietly shooing their children toward their homes and to bed. Loo-kani approached Hannah and spoke to her, waiting for Soo-shani to translate.

"She is wondering if you would like to go to sleep now Hannah," Soo-shani said.

Suddenly beyond exhausted at the long and wondrous day that she had had, Hannah nodded her head and stood to her feet.

Loo-kani helped Soo-shani up and the three of them walked to a small hut that stood near the base of the hill with Luna close behind them. The door of the hut was basically a curtain fastened to the top of the doorway. When she walked into the hut, Hannah's eyes scanned its interior, taking everything in. There was a small pit in the center that held a warm, crackling fire which gave light to the rest of the hut. The walls were made of wood and clay, and they were completely bare.

There were two beds made up on the floor. Hannah wondered who she was rooming with until Soo-shani spoke up.

"You will be sleeping with me tonight Hannah. Make yourself comfortable."

Loo-kani spoke again to Hannah and Soo-shani translated,

"Is there anything else that you need?"

Hannah shook her head, "No. Thank you for everything."

When Soo-shani told Loo-kani what Hannah had said, she smiled at Hannah and said,

"Vespen Hannah," before exiting the hut.

Hannah turned to Soo-shani and asked, "What does 'vespen' mean?"

"It means blessings," Soo-shani replied as she sank down onto her bed.

Hannah walked around the fire to the other bed and sat down, stretching her hands and feet toward the fire's warmth. Soo-shani had already laid down, her eyes slowly drifting closed. Wanting to say goodnight to Luna, Hannah stood back up and walked out the curtained doorway, being careful not to wake up Soo-shani. Luna was grazing on the lush green grass that was growing all around the hut. She nickered when she saw Hannah coming up towards her and tossed her head in the air, her long mane catching the breeze.

"Hello Luna," Hannah whispered to her.

Luna looked deep into Hannah's eyes, watching her like she always did. Hannah wondered what Luna was thinking about. She always seemed so thoughtful and observant, her liquid brown eyes taking in everything, never missing a moment. Luna nuzzled Hannah's hair before looking up to the sky. Following her gaze, Hannah's jaw dropped at the sight she beheld. It seemed as if every inch of sky was covered with brilliant and pure white specks of light. Shooting stars raced each other through the darkness and constellations danced with each other around the moon.

Hannah couldn't tear her gaze away from the night sky. It almost seemed as if she was seeing it in a different way tonight. Luna brought her back to earth when she softly butted Hannah with the side of her big head, being careful not to hit her with the lovely horn on her forehead. Hannah rubbed Luna's nose before wrapping her arms around her friend's neck. Taking a deep breath, she stepped back, weariness beginning to overtake her small body. She had had a long and full day and needed to get to bed.

Hannah blew Luna one last kiss goodnight before walking back into Soo-shani's hut. The fire was beginning to die down, but it was still plenty warm. She walked around the hut to her bed, being extra cautious so as not to disturb Soo-shani, who was sleeping soundly. The blankets that Loo-kani had placed on her bed were of lovely grays and browns woven into swirling patterns that stretched across the entire thing.

Smiling to herself, Hannah slipped between the covers and snuggled herself up tight. She had had such a long day. Feeling safe and warm, her eyes began to drift shut and she fell into a deep and sweet slumber.

Chapter 9

"Time to wake up Hannah," Soo-shani called through the darkness. Hannah slowly opened her eyes and blinked rapidly trying to rid her mind of the sleepy fog that threatened to put her back to sleep. Looking up at Soo-shani, Hannah saw that Chief Li-kani and Loo-kani were both standing there with her, watching her.

"What's going on?" Hannah asked.

"It's time for you to be joined with our tribe Hannah," Soo-shani stated simply.

Hannah's eyes widened and she scanned the faces of the chief and his daughter. They did not appear to be joking in the least. Their faces were hard as stone, their eyes set in a determined way.

"But I want to go home!" Hannah exclaimed, her beautiful blue eyes beginning to fill with tears. She sat up in bed and watched everyone intently.

"Hush now child. This is no time to cry. You should have thought about that before eating our food and wearing our clothes. You can never go home now," Soo-shani said as Loo-kani and the chief each grabbed one of Hannah's arms. Hannah tried to kick and fight, but some unknown force was holding her in place as they dragged her out of the hut.

"Luna!" Hannah called out desperately. "Luna!" There was no answer.

"Luna is gone, Hannah. She chose wrong and is no longer here to protect you," Soo-shani said coldly. "It is time for the ceremony."

Looking around, Hannah saw all the people surrounding the fire pit in the center of the village. They were chanting something in their language, their faces watching her with a dark and calloused look in their *eyes. Hannah didn't know what they were about to do, but it couldn't be good.*

Suddenly, she recognized two of the people in the crowd. Pete and Joe! What were they doing here? Terror gripped her as she tried even harder to fight the rock-solid grip that the chief and his daughter had on her arms.

"Someone help me!" Hannah cried out.

"Don't fight it Hannah." A familiar voice behind her caused her to swing her head around. Father? With Mother next to him?

"Father! Please help me!"

"Hannah, this must be done. Do not fight it."

No! How could Father be on the side of these savage people?

The closer she got to the fire, the louder the people got in their chant.

"No!" Hannah cried out again. "Please no!"

Hannah shot up straight in bed, her eyes wide and her heart beating double time. She snapped her head over to look at Soo-shani who was still sleeping atop her bed. Taking in deep gulps of air, Hannah tried to calm herself while thinking about her dream. Was it a warning? What if the people really did want to keep her there forever? She just couldn't stay! Making a frantic decision, Hannah jumped up out of bed, folded the blanket over neatly and crept out of the tiny hut.

The moon was full, shining itself on Hannah's silky blonde hair and the sky was beginning to lighten with the coming sunrise. Scanning the hillside, Hannah spotted Luna grazing on the lush grass. Luna raised her head to see Hannah making her way over and began to walk towards the girl. Reaching Luna, Hannah threw her arms around the unicorn and began to cry again. She had been crying so much these past couple of days that it was a wonder that there were any tears left.

"We have to leave Luna," Hannah whimpered into Luna's mane.

Luna snorted and nuzzled Hannah's hair in response.

"Come on, let's go," Hannah said.

Releasing Luna from her embrace, Hannah began to walk up the hill, heading in the direction from which she had come with Noo-ashi.

Luna snorted again and didn't move, her big eyes asking a thousand questions.

"Come on Luna! We have to leave! These people are going to make me stay here forever and I can't do that!" Hannah said desperately. She began her climb again, looking back to see if Luna was going to follow her. To her relief, the unicorn had started taking small steps towards her, slowly making her way up the hill.

Once Hannah reached the top of the hill, she began to move faster through the Dark Woods in the direction she presumed would lead her back to the waterfall. As quickly as she could, she stepped over rocks and tree roots. Her mind was a flurry of thoughts and worries. Would the Sephramin try to follow her and take her back to their village? What if she never found her way back and ended up dying in these woods? What would become of her and Luna?

Hannah pushed her doubts out of her mind as she continued to move forward. The early dawn cast a new light on the woods and the dew on ground twinkled like drops of starlight. Little critters scurried to their holes as she and Luna walked by and birds poured out their little hearts in song, singing for the sunrise. A gentle breeze blew and pulled Hannah's blonde hair loose from its braid. The small tendrils brushed against her cheeks and eyelashes.

Luna's soft footfalls were almost noiseless on the forest floor. Her eyes scanned the trees, noticing any movement that presented itself. Her long mane and tail barely brushed the fallen leaves that covered their path. Hannah walked close by her, Luna's tall body a comforting presence as they walked through unknown territory. The sound of rushing water was their only guide as the duo made their way toward the waterfall.

The sun was on its way up over the hill as Hannah finally reached the waterfall. After finding the hidden entrance, she grabbed Luna's mane and slowly walked into the damp darkness. The light got brighter as they got closer to the other side and the ground got more slippery.

Hannah's moccasins gripped the ground pretty well, but she lost her footing a few times. Hannah's grip on Luna got tighter when they neared the edge of the ledge under the waterfall.

Then suddenly, without warning, Hannah's feet slid out from under her and she slipped off the edge. The roar of the water filled her ears and she screamed. Still holding onto Luna's mane, she dangled over the ledge. Drops of water rolled through her hair and into her eyes causing her vision to become blurry. Luna whinnied and braced herself, her eyes filled with fear. Hannah looked right at Luna and screamed, "Help me Luna! Help me please!" The panic in her heart increased as her grip loosened on Luna's mane. There was nothing either of them could do.

With her fingers drained of their strength, Hannah lost her grip on Luna's mane and tumbled over the ledge into the gushing torrent of water. The weight of the water took her breath away and felt like it bruised every inch of her body. Hannah crashed into the river below the waterfall and was pushed into the heavy current.

Her mind racing, Hannah began to swim to the surface. Her lungs were burning in her chest and the blood in her temples was pounding like a drum. Her feet caught on a rock on the river bottom and, using the last of her strength, Hannah pushed off towards the top of her watery prison. Gasping for oxygen, Hannah finally broke through the surface of the river. The water running in her eyes destroyed any chance of her seeing a way out. The river rapids were strong and steady, smashing Hannah's body into every rock and branch that came in her way. She tried frantically to grab onto anything that might save her, but there was nothing that was strong enough to hold her.

Hannah was unable to think clearly. Her strength was gone, and she was at the mercy of the river. She felt her body go limp as she gave in to the water. Blackness started overtaking her and she welcomed it as the pain in her body began to dissipate. Just before she lost consciousness, a loud horse's squeal filled the air around her, cutting through the sound of the water. *Maybe Luna will save me,* Hannah thought as she blacked out.

Chapter 10

She couldn't get away from the darkness. Hannah ran until her heart felt like bursting and still hadn't managed to escape it. "Help me!" She called out desperately. "Please! Someone help me! It's going to get me!" Hannah ran further into the woods surrounding her. The darkness seemed to close in from all sides with no escape. The sounds of roaring winds followed her and drowned out any hope she had left. She was forced to stop when a dark shadowy figure appeared in front of her. It seemed to mock Hannah with its presence, taunting her with its every movement. A dark, menacing laugh came from behind her, and two more shadowy figures began to approach her. Hannah wanted to cover her eyes, but some unseen force held her arms down and she watched in horror as the shadows came closer and closer. Their arms were raised up in preparation to strike and Hannah braced for impact.

Then suddenly from the midst of the darkness, a clear whistle broke through the noise and the living darkness came to a halt. The three figures were frozen in time as a tiny ball of pure white light began to grow in the woods directly in front of Hannah. It got closer and closer, and as it got closer it grew. As it moved through the forest, seemingly in slow motion, the darkness was forced to retreat, not being able to withstand the force of the light. A lovely, melodious sound reached Hannah's ears as the light began to take a form. The sound felt like angels singing and church bells ringing, yet it was quiet and comforting, and soothed her battered soul. Hannah had never heard anything like it before.

All at once, light exploded from the ball as it took its final form. It was a unicorn, but Hannah didn't know how to describe it. Its likeness was similar to Luna's, but at the same time, it was completely different. Something about it was even more beautiful and majestic, though she didn't know why. Its body was sleek, shimmering in the pure white light that radiated from its magnificent horn. The unicorn's eyes met with Hannah as it began to gallop around her, creating a larger and larger sphere of light, erasing any lingering darkness.

Finally satisfied with its work, the unicorn began to run back toward Hannah. It got closer and closer without slowing down. If it were any other time, Hannah would have been afraid, but something about this creature gave her the most incredible feeling of peace and hope. The unicorn got brighter and brighter as it ran, finally turning into a globe of white light that collided with her, disappearing into her chest. It wasn't pain that Hannah felt though. It was life. Her eyes drifted closed in blessed slumber as she sank down to the grassy forest floor...

Hannah's eyes fluttered open as pain began to flood her body. Every inch of her small frame was aching from her plight in the river and her head throbbed. In her attempt to take in a breath, she found that she couldn't. Panicking, Hannah turned over to her side and watched as water began to flood from her mouth. The small breath that she took began a coughing fit that racked her whole body, causing the pain to increase.

Her breaths were coming in slowly and shakily, but they were coming. Hannah opened her eyes to blurry vision. The light from the sun was streaming through the branches of the trees above her head. A light breeze rustled the leaves and the wisps of hair around her face. She blinked again, trying to steady her vision. The birds in the trees seemed to be singing lullabies to her and the river's roar was more like a gentle hush. Hannah didn't want to wake up, but the pain in her body was gradually growing more and more concerning.

Finally coming to her bearings, Hannah slowly turned her head all around and scanned her surroundings. The river was still running on her left and the forest was on her right. The ground that she was lying on was lush green grass with tiny white flowers dotting the earth like snowflakes. Her new shoes were nowhere to be found, the cool breeze on her feet sending shivers up her spine.

Moving with extreme caution, Hannah sat up and blinked rapidly, trying to make her world stop spinning. The river beside her lost its fuzziness and her mind cleared as she remembered what had happened. Not wanting to get up just yet, Hannah laid back down on the soft grass trying to will her tired muscles to stop aching. Questions started flowing through her mind, like how did she get out of the river? What happened while she was unconscious? Did she almost die? Where was Luna? Remembering the squeal she had heard before submitting to the darkness, Hannah wondered if it was Luna who had made the sound.

Mustering up the strength to sit up once again, Hannah rolled onto her side and slowly eased herself up with her arms. Feeling pain in her hand, she began to examine it, finding that her left thumb was swollen and purple, sitting at a weird angle. The sight of it made her stomach queasy and her head spin. She looked away, ignoring the pain and moved on to check the rest of her body. Her whole right arm and most of her left arm was covered in purple and blue bruises and she was missing the fingernail of her right middle finger, most likely from when she was trying to claw her way out of the river.

Hannah reached to the back of her head and yelped when she ran her fingers over a large bump on her skull. It wasn't bleeding, but her head was throbbing. She ran her hands down her legs, praying that there weren't any broken bones. Not feeling any sort of abnormality, she tried to stand up. Suddenly feeling woozy and unstable on her wobbly legs, she sat back down, willing away the nausea that threatened to take over.

If she wasn't in so much pain, she might actually have enjoyed the view she had of the river and the bank. Hannah stretched her legs out and tried to soothe her aching muscles. The longer she sat there, the better she began to feel. Her stomach had started to growl and she was extremely thirsty, but Hannah was not willing to go near the river. If she fell in again, she wasn't sure if she would ever get out of the raging current. The calmness of the river and the lovely sounds the forest emitted was suddenly brought to a halt when Hannah came to the realization that she had no idea where she was. She wasn't even sure if she was on the right side of the river!

The pain in her head increased as her thoughts became more frenzied. Her stomach growled reminding her that she hadn't eaten for hours, she was parched of thirst, and had no place to go. It was more than enough to put her off the edge and Hannah found herself slipping back into the darkness that wooed her with its calm serenity. Her body fell back onto the ground, but she didn't feel a thing. She lay on the banks of the river, once again unconscious.

As she lay there, the sun began to set and the forest around her came alive. Curious little creatures approached her cautiously, wondering what this strange thing was and what it was doing out in the woods. The sun winked goodnight to the world and the moon snuck up into the heavens, the stars swirling in a brilliant, lovely dance around it. Fireflies stepped into the darkness and tried to coax the young girl from slumber, but she would not be awakened. The night sounds created a symphony of sound, lulling the earth into a trance. Hannah was vulnerable in the dark, but the creatures of the wood kept a watchful eye on her, keeping her from harm.

Late in the unusually warm spring night, Hannah finally woke up. Her eyes flew

open and her vision was filled with a seemingly holy light given by the stars and the moon. Tears filled her eyes and she began to cry. She was sure this is where she would die. Her body still ached and her head still throbbed from the rushing river. Nothing in her wanted to move, so she laid there, tears falling into the damp grass and sorrow filling her heart. She cried herself to sleep, still exhausted from the river. When she woke again, the sun was peeking over the horizon, a new day beginning.

The sound of the river and the birds singing brought little comfort, but her eyes widened as a new sound reached her ears. Whispers in the wind, voices that pierced her heart with fear darted through the woods and hit her with a terrifying memory of the dark back room of a dusty shack. She wanted to stand and run as far away from them as she could, but her body wasn't listening to her brain. Her muscles were so stiff that she couldn't move save for stretching her neck to scan the woods up and down the river. A slight rustling of the bushes caused her head to snap to the right. A small rabbit darted out of the woods and almost ran into her before running upstream, reentering the forest for safety.

The voices were no longer whispers in the wind, but full-fledged arguments and conversations that carried to where she was lying. The ground seemed to shake with the weight of heavy feet. They were not even trying to be quiet. Hannah closed her eyes and began to pray. Her body couldn't handle any more rough action and she was afraid of what the two men would do to her when they found her. It was inevitable at this point. They were going to find her and she had no place to hide. Tears spilled from her eyes as she squeezed them shut in an attempt to block out the horrible memory of them, but they came crashing through the bushes and halted at the sight of her.

Chapter 11

“Well well well, look what we have here...” Joe remarked smugly.

Hannah couldn't stop the flow of tears and she began to sob.

“Maybe this will teach you not to run from us again. My word, look at her Pete. She's covered in bruises. And what in the world is she wearing?”

“How should I know? All women's clothes look the same.” He turned to Hannah and asked, “Did you fall into the river?” She didn't say a word, but turned her head away from the two men. Joe closed the gap between them, grabbed her face in his hands and repeated, “Did you fall into the river? Answer us!” He raised his hand to strike her, but Pete stopped him.

“She's hurt enough as it is Joe.”

Joe tore his hand away from Pete and said slowly and menacingly, “Do not touch me again.” The anger in his eyes was enough to scare the life out of Hannah. When he turned back towards her, she cringed, expecting a striking blow.

“Last chance princess. Did you fall into the river?” Joe asked almost mockingly.

Afraid of what he might do, Hannah nodded slowly, her body still aching from the bruises. Pete, slightly more concerned for her than Joe was, walked around her and then knelt down. He picked up her left hand and began to examine her thumb.

“Is it broken?” Joe asked Pete, more out of curiosity than concern.

“I don't think so. It looks like it's just out of place.” He turned his attention to Hannah and said, “This is going to hurt for a second, but it will feel better once I put it back in place.” Hannah didn't care anymore. How could it hurt more than it did now? She shut her eyes as Pete gently pulled on her thumb and moved it back to its correct spot. A sickening crack echoed in the clearing and she cried out in pain. Hannah wretched her hand away from Pete and curled up in a ball, her bones and muscles groaning from the effort. She just wanted them to go away and leave her alone. Why were there such bad men in this world? The tears had not stopped flowing and now they came with more fervor than before.

"Come on kid. We're bringing you back to your parents, as long as they pay up," Joe said with a sneer.

"She can't walk Joe. Look at her. She can barely move," Pete protested.

"Well, I'm not carrying her, so either she walks, or you carry her," Joe retorted.

Pete turned his attention back to Hannah and asked, "Can you walk?"

Hannah looked up into his golden eyes and saw genuine concern for her in their depths. She shook her head and managed to choke out a *no* through her sobs. In response, Pete gently placed one arm behind her shoulders and the other behind her knees as he picked her up. Hannah put her arms around his neck and cried into his shirt. She still hated both of them, but Pete was better than Joe. He seemed to care at least a little bit about her wellbeing, even in the shack. He was the one that had insisted on feeding her and giving her water.

Joe led the way as Pete carried her back along the crude path that he and Joe had made through the woods. Even after sleeping for as long as she did, Hannah was still exhausted and didn't put up a fight as they moved through the trees. Her legs bobbed to the rhythm of Pete's gait and her head lobbed to one side as she began to drift off into sleep again. Before she gave in to slumber though, she heard Joe stop and say, "What do you think that Steven is going to do to us if he sees her like this?..." Suddenly, Hannah wasn't tired anymore. She kept her eyes shut, but listened intently to their conversation.

"Why does that matter? He will never find us again. With the money, we can leave this wretched island and go somewhere warm," Pete answered.

"But to leave, we will have to go through the port, and he practically owns the port."

"Then we'll find another way to leave. Let's just get this over with."

"No Pete, you don't get it. If we bring back his daughter looking like a drowned and beaten kitten, he will kill us both."

"Well, what should we do then?"

"I think we should kill her and tell Steven that she ran away from us, fell into the river, and drowned."

"Look Joe, I didn't sign up for murder. I may be a thief, but I am not a monster. We are going to take her back to her father and that is final. She can tell him herself that she fell into the river and barely survived," Pete ended with a *humph* and began walking again.

"You are not the one in charge here Petey. Don't you dare walk away from me," Joe snarled. Pete spun around and Hannah's eyes shot open just in time to see Joe pull a revolver out of the waistband of his pants.

"Now hold her still," Joe said to Hannah's despair.

She panicked and, without warning, kicked free of Pete's grip. She fell on the ground at his feet, but was up again in a heartbeat, running through the woods. She didn't care where, she just had to get away. They couldn't catch her again.

"You softy! I knew she could walk!" Joe yelled. "Just catch her!"

Footsteps sounded loudly behind her as she pushed herself to run faster and faster. The wind moved with her, giving her breath to keep moving and the trees made a pathway for her. Their branches moved with the wind and their leaves cheered her on. The birds that flew alongside her sang encouragement, as if their songs could give her strength. It seemed as if the entire woods was helping her to escape until she tripped on an old, dried-up stump and tumbled head over heels, landing with a root pressed into her back.

The world got fuzzy and started to spin, but instead of giving into the dark like she had before, Hannah looked up to the heavens and uttered a single word, "Help." Instantly, her grandfather's voice from her dream came back to her saying, "*They are coming Hannah. Don't be afraid.*" She thought about how brave and strong her grandfather had been and how he had not given up the fight, even when he had no way out. Anger began to find its way into her heart along with a strong determination to fight back. They could not do this to her. She was stronger than this and she knew it. If she had learned anything from Grandfather's stories, it was that there was always strength left. Even when all hope was gone, there was still hope left. She clung to that hope as she set her face like granite.

Hannah stood to her feet, not willing to run any further, and waited for her captors to break through the trees. Their crashing and yelling was a dead giveaway to where they were. She pushed all fear out of her and instead clung to the hope that she would survive to see her parents again because someone would find her and save her. Pete came bursting through the line of trees first, being in better shape than Joe, but he stopped at the sight of her. She didn't know it, but the sun shone through the lingering morning mist and gave her the appearance of having wings. Her blonde hair was blowing angelically in the wind and her eyes shone with a fire that was not of this world. When Joe broke through, his eyes widened, and he too stopped to watch her. Hannah lifted her head up high, clenched her fists, and said, "You will not touch me again. I was chosen by a star, and once chosen by a star, you are chosen forever."

Joe smirked and Pete rolled his eyes at her statement. In sync with each other, both men began walking through the fallen leaves to reach her. She watched as Joe crushed a tiny white flower with his big, clunky foot and a small dot of fear crept into her heart

Suddenly, to her surprise, Pete stopped Joe and pointed behind Hannah, his jaw dropping. Hannah peeked over her shoulder and almost squealed with joy. Luna! She came back! Her silky white mane and tail flying like banners in the wind. Her nostrils were flared and her head pulsed with the rhythm of her gallop. Luna was moving with fury through the woods towards Hannah and her captors, determination in every stride. Her gentle eyes were now filled with fiery anger and the melodious sound of even hoofbeats were like a healing salve to Hannah's weary soul.

Luna didn't stop as she neared Hannah, rather she sped up, going faster and faster, her slender horn aiming right at Pete.

Chapter 12

Hannah didn't know what to do as she sank to the forest floor, watching. Joe yelled at Pete to get out of the way and Pete jumped to the side. When Luna hit him with her horn, she only pierced his shoulder. His cry of pain echoed in the woods and ended with a thud as Luna tossed him off her horn, banging him against a tree. When Hannah looked at his face, he seemed to be unconscious. Joe had started running past Hannah to the left and was trying to get away through the woods, jumping over fallen trees and rocks. Luna stopped and turned around, pawing the ground with her hoof and shaking her head. She reared up on two hind legs, let out a whinny and began running back at Joe, her head down and horn parallel to the ground, the fire still raging in her eyes. Joe heard her coming and spun around, his face a set decision. Hannah watched in horror as Joe reached behind him and pulled out his revolver from his waistband. Her eyes widened with fear and she screamed as he pulled the trigger, his barrel pointing right at Luna.

To Hannah, everything was suddenly moving in slow motion. Joe pulled the trigger on his gun, aiming at Luna as she charged at him. His bullet connected with her chest, but she didn't stop, her determination to protect Hannah stronger than the pain in her body. Her horn surged into his stomach and she flung him into the bushes, her horn and forehead dripping red from his blood. Hannah's hands went up and covered her mouth in shock, but spun around when she heard a sound behind her. Pete had gotten up and was trying to stop his shoulder from bleeding. Luna locked eyes with him and seemingly stared him down. His eyes widened and he turned, frantically running through the woods, tripping on roots and getting wrapped up in briars. Luna didn't look away from him until he was out of sight.

She turned to face Hannah and Hannah gasped at the wound on her chest. Blood was running bright red down Luna's leg and staining the ground in its flow. Luna made her way over to Hannah, moving slower and slower until she collapsed into the dirt. Hannah's heart dropped into her stomach and she scrambled over to where Luna had fallen.

"Oh Luna." Hannah whispered. Luna nickered softly at Hannah and closed her eyes. Hannah sat down on the ground next to Luna and placed her hand on the unicorn's white neck.

With some effort, Hannah picked up Luna's strong head and placed it in her lap, stroking her beautiful neck and humming the song that Soo-shani had sung the night

before. Tears fell from her eyes and onto Luna's lovely neck and mane as she began to sing new words to the song as they flowed from her heart.

Luna my friend thank you from my heart
You saved me from the men who wished me harm
Now I release you to your Maker's Hand
I will not forget you, the one who helped me stand.

"You saved me Luna," Hannah whispered into her ear. Luna's eyes were closed and she was bleeding all over, but she was still breathing and managed to make a soft noise in her throat. Hannah clung to Luna and continued to sing to her through her sobs, trying to calm herself and the unicorn. What was she supposed to do? There was just so much blood. The thought of losing Luna after such a short time broke Hannah's heart and caused her to cry even more.

Hannah didn't know how long she sat there stroking Luna's forehead, but the sun was starting to go down and Luna's breathing was slowing. Hannah watched in despair as Luna's eyes fluttered shut and she wheezed out a final breath. There were no more knickers, no swirling brown eyes watching her, and no loving nuzzles. Hannah leaned over Luna's lifeless body and cried into her neck, so tired and heartbroken that she fell asleep within minutes.

HANNAH'S EYES OPENED, blinking against the bright light that surrounded her. She looked down, expecting to see Luna, dead, right next to her, but she was gone. Looking around her frantically, Hannah squinted at the light, realizing that she couldn't see anything because of how bright it was. Her attention was drawn to the space in front of her as the light seemingly parted for something making its way toward her. It was the big unicorn that she had seen after she fell into the river! It was coming straight towards her again, but as it got closer, it began to change form.

Confused, Hannah watched as the glorious unicorn transformed into a man, tall and strong, clothed in white. He had a golden crown on his head and his eyes were an incomparable blue. The closest she could get to describing them was that they were like the sky had finally met the ocean and the two had collided, mixing together in the loveliest of ways. In her heart, she knew that this was the man that Soo-shani had sung about. He was the one who sent the unicorns to earth. Hannah heard a soft nicker behind her and spun around, her jaw dropping in shock as Luna appeared from the forest. She nodded her head at Hannah and walked right past her into the arms of the man waiting for her.

The man looked at Hannah and said, "Thank you." The simple words cut Hannah to the depths and she began to cry, but for once, the tears were happy tears. Luna and the man began to walk away, back where the man had come from. As they walked, the man slowly turned back into a unicorn, making Luna look like a baby. Luna looked back at Hannah one last time, her eyes seeming to say that she was going to be alright. Then she turned and began to gallop with the larger unicorn until they disappeared into the light.

HANNAH AWOKE SEVERAL hours later, the forest floor damp beneath her clothes and the sun warm on her face as it flitted in and out of the clouds. She blinked a few times, allowing her eyes to adjust to the light and then she remembered everything. Hannah's eyes dropped down to the ground and widened when she saw that Luna wasn't there! She spun around frantically trying to figure out what had happened when she was asleep. As if sensing her panic, the sun fell behind a cloud, dimming the light in the forest. Who would have taken a dead unicorn and left her? Pete was the only one who might have done something, but he was very wounded. Besides, he wasn't after Luna, he was after her. Tears began to fill Hannah's lovely eyes once more and began to drip on the mossy ground as she hung her head. The sun began to peek out from behind the white puffy clouds in the sky and it's light danced across something lying on the ground beside her. Hiding underneath the leaves that graced the forest floor was a long, slender unicorn horn. It reflected every color of the rainbow and glistened with the dew from the damp ground.

Hannah's eyes widened as she slowly picked up the horn from the ground. Had her dream come true? Did that man really come get Luna while she was sleeping? What else could have happened to her? A unicorn is not easy to move, and Hannah would have woken up if someone moved Luna. Her head started to hurt as she searched for an explanation. The birds sang around her as they bounced from tree to tree and the small woodland creatures peeked curiously at her from their hiding places. Hannah slowly stood to her feet and gazed up at the canopy of trees above her. In her heart, she knew that Luna was back with her brothers and sisters dancing among the stars.

Her whimsical musings were cut short by a sharp sound through the trees on her right. Hannah's breath caught in her throat and she froze. How much more must she endure before she could finally breathe easily? But her fears were transformed into hope when she heard a familiar voice shouting, "Hannah! Hannah!"

"I'm here!" Hannah yelled back.

Chapter 13

Recognizing her grandfather's voice, relief flooded her soul and she cried out, "I'm over here! I'm over here!"

The unicorn horn still in her hand, she plunged into the forest towards the sound of his voice. Breaking through the brush, she spotted him and her heart lifted into the sky, soaring with the birds.

"Grandfather!" She yelled as she sprinted to him.

"Hannah!" He yelled back, his arms wide open to catch her.

Hannah slammed into his chest, wrapped her arms around his middle and began to cry.

"Oh Grandfather! I thought I would never see you again!" She managed to choke out between the sobs.

Grandfather stroked her hair and said, "Shhh. It's okay. I'm here now."

They stood there for a while, Hannah clinging to him like she would never hold him again. As her tears slowed, Grandfather asked, "We got a ransom note, but when we brought the money, no one showed up. What happened?"

Hannah explained that after she had been taken, the two men tied her up in a dark and damp cabin deep in the woods. She had managed to escape but then had gotten lost in the woods when they started chasing her. As she told her story, her grandfather noticed the horn in her hand. His eyes widened and he whispered breathlessly, "What is that!?"

Hannah smiled up at him and said simply, "It's a unicorn horn."

Grandfather kneeled down in front of her and placed his hands on her shoulders, looking her right in the eye.

"You found a unicorn horn? In the woods?" he asked, his eyes searching hers for an answer.

Hannah smiled and chuckled before replying, "No silly. I found a *unicorn* in the woods." Grandfather sat there, speechless as Hannah continued. "Actually, she found me when I was lost. She kept me warm all night. Her name was Luna. She saved me again when those two guys found me." Her face fell as she recounted Luna's sacrifice. "That's how she died. One of them was going to shoot me, but she ran right at him and pushed her horn into his belly right after he shot her," Hannah cast her eyes downward to the ground as the memory of Luna's death came rushing back at her again. Tears threatened to begin again as Grandfather shook her slightly.

"Where is she now Hannah? What did you do with her body? How did you get her horn?" Grandfather's questions came fast and he looked at her with eager anticipation.

"It was on the ground when I woke up. The man from Soo-shani's song came and took Luna away. She looked really happy to be with him."

Grandfather plopped down on the ground and ran his hand through his hair, his face still holding a shocked expression.

"I don't even know what to say Hannah. How could this have all happened?" he asked. "And who is Soo-shani?"

"Soo-shani is part of the Sephramin tribe that lives on the other side of the waterfall. She used to live in Anadulan with everyone else, but when her family died, she wandered into the woods until someone from the tribe found her. She's blind," Hannah stated bluntly.

Upon hearing about the Sephramin tribe, Grandfather looked surprised.

"You found the Sephramin's?" he asked slowly.

Hannah looked puzzled.

"What's the matter? Is something wrong?" she asked inquisitively. Grandfather opened his mouth to speak when there was a rustle in the bushes to their right.

"Get behind me," Grandfather spoke sharply to Hannah. She rushed behind him and clung to him as they waited for whatever was in the bushes to appear.

Suddenly, without warning, they were surrounded by Sephramin warriors. They were painted with war paint and their hair was braided down their backs, away from their faces. The sun glinted off their spears and their piercing eyes sent shivers down Hannah's spine. They began talking to each other in their native tongue, pointing at Grandfather as their voices got louder and more intense. Grandfather was nervously scanning the Sephramins when they stopped talking and raised their spear towards him.

"No!" Hannah cried. "He's my grandfather! He won't hurt anyone!"

But her words were in vain. They had no idea what she was saying. In fact, her panicked tone seemed to upset them even more. The biggest one standing in front of Grandfather yelled out something and Hannah closed her eyes.

To her surprise, she heard another voice. When she opened her eyes, Chief Li-kani was standing in front of Grandfather, his hand holding down the biggest warrior's spear. He locked eyes with Grandfather and the two of them broke into a smile. Chief Li-kani held out his hand to Grandfather and they grasped forearms. Hannah was so confused. How did Grandfather know Chief Li-kani?

"My old friend," Grandfather said with joy in his voice.

"Friend," Chief Li-kani replied. The Chief turned to Hannah with a smile on his face and repeated the word.

"Friend."

Hannah felt her fear slipping away and replied, "Friend."

Chief Li-kani motioned for Hannah and Grandfather to follow him and he, along with his warriors, led the two of them back through the woods to the waterfall. Grandfather whistled for Dandy, his gorgeous gelding, who trotted through the woods to him. He put Hannah up onto the horse and began to lead them after the chief and his warriors.

"Grandfather," Hannah asked, puzzled. "How do you know Chief Li-kani?"

Grandfather smiled at her, but she could tell that he was also sad.

"I fell in love with a woman from their tribe when I first came here many years ago. She happened to be the chief's sister. We got married soon after and began a life together, but the people that I came here with began to get suspicious of my disappearance." Grandfather sighed and lowered his eyes. "In order to protect my wife and our baby on the way, I decided that I would leave, at least for a little bit to keep everyone else away from my new life. After I left, my wife Sah-sheena couldn't bear to be away from me. It broke her heart. When I finally returned, I found that she had gone into labor early and had died along with the baby. I couldn't stay there after I lost her. The pain was too great."

Grandfather seemed to be in a trance, as if he was remembering her and their time together. Hannah watched the memories float through his eyes, wondering what they might be. He turned his head to look at Hannah and asked out of the blue, "Who did you say took Luna away?"

"The man that Soo-shani sang about in her song. The One who sent the unicorns to earth. He was the One who took her back into the sky with him. Now she can run with her brothers and sisters and play with the moon."

Grandfather looked confused and said, "I don't understand Hannah. Who exactly was this man?"

"The man who made the unicorns. Their Creator," Hannah stated again with a shrug of her shoulders.

After walking back over the miles the river had swept Hannah away, the troop finally made it to the waterfall. The memory of her fall rushed back into her mind and Hannah grabbed the arm of one of the warriors without even thinking. Instead of brushing her away, the warrior took her hand and smiled at her, motioning and gently tugging her forward through the tunnel. She managed a smile back at him and let him guide her over the slippery rocks. Before she knew it, they were back in the lovely clearing, the Sephramin village just down the hill.

When the children saw them crest the hill, they whooped and hollered, running at them and speaking with excited voices.

"Hannah?" a familiar voice spoke through the noise.

"Soo-shani!" Hannah yelled. Her heart rose into her throat as she realized the worry she must have caused the older woman. Hannah ran down the hill to Soo-shani, stopping just short of her.

"Soo-shani, I'm so sorry that I ran away," she blubbered. "I just had a really bad nightmare and got so scared and…"

"Oh, hush child," Soo-shani chided as she reached for her. "Come here. No one here is upset with you."

"But Luna's dead and it's all my fault!" Hannah sobbed as she wrapped her arms around the grandmotherly woman. "If I hadn't left, those bad guys wouldn't have found me, and she wouldn't have needed to rescue me. I killed her Soo-shani!" Hannah cried into Soo-shani's shawl, taking comfort in her arms.

"Unicorns are not like other creatures Hannah," Soo-shani said comfortingly as she stroked Hannah's windblown hair. "They choose the one they will walk with and they choose when they will sacrifice themselves. Luna could have stopped you or chosen to find a different way to save you, but she decided that she was going to sacrifice herself for you. She *chose* to give her life, you didn't take it. Don't hold this regret or heartache in your heart. Remember that she was made to be with her Maker, and she was missing Him."

Hannah remembered her dream of Luna and the man and remembered how happy Luna looked as she walked off with the larger unicorn. The memory made her heart warm and her tears began to slow. It was almost as if she could hear Luna speaking to her saying she was happy and whole. When she finally let go of Soo-shani, Hannah realized that almost the entire village was watching her, including Grandfather. He opened his arms to her and Hannah gladly welcomed the comfort.

"I think that we should go home," Grandfather stated simply.

Hannah nodded her head in agreement, still in his arms. To her surprise, Grandfather began speaking to the chief in the Sephramin language. When he was finished speaking, the chief motioned to his daughter who brought Hannah her nightgown, the one she had been kidnapped in. It had been scrubbed and washed until there were only a few small grass stains left on it.

"You need to change out of the clothes that they gave you. This village is a secret from the rest of the island, and they want to keep it that way. If the Anadulan people found out about the Sephramin, they would take over and enforce their ways onto every villager, and we don't want that."

The chief nodded and spoke again, motioning to his daughter and another woman standing next to her.

"The chief also want's you to go with their healer. You have quite a bump on the back of your head and she wants to make sure that you're okay," Grandfather translated.

Hannah nodded her head and turned to Loo-kani and the healer who led her to a tent a few feet away. A mere ten minutes later, Hannah emerged again, smelling of sweet oils and dressed in her nightgown again. She turned to her grandfather and said, "I'm ready to go home." Home. The thought of it made her heart well up inside. Grandfather nodded at her and replied, "Let's say goodbye then."

Hannah turned to her new friends and began to bid them each farewell. When she got to Soo-shani, her heart began to sadden and the tears she had been holding back spilled over. Over the course of one day, she had grown very fond of the older woman.

"Thank you for everything Soo-shani. I wish you were my grandmother and I could come visit you every day." Hannah's voice broke in the middle of her sentence and Soo-shani reached for her. Hannah willingly walked into her arms and hugged her with everything she had.

Soo-shani released her and took Hannah's face in her hands.

"Never forget, dear one, you are a chosen one of the stars. Once chosen by a star, you are chosen forever. Luna and her Maker, along with all her brothers and sisters will be watching over you forever. Do not walk in fear, but walk in strength, love, and peace. Honor Luna's memory, but don't let your heart be troubled."

Soo-shani's words settled deep into Hannah's heart and she knew that they would never be forgotten. Soo-shani brought Hannah's forehead to her own and whispered, "Goodbye my child."

Hannah hugged her one last time before turning to her grandfather, hand held out. He grasped it and led her to Dandy, who nickered at the sight of them. Grandfather lifted her up onto his horse and then climbed up behind her, grasping the reins.

"Vespen!" He shouted at the tribe as they took off up the hill.

Hannah waved at them as they shouted back, "Vespen Hannah! Vespen Charles!"

Chapter 14

Hannah felt so safe in Grandfather's arms that she began to nod off, the even rhythm of Dandy's gait like a lullaby in motion. She didn't even remember passing through the waterfall tunnel or when they reached the edge of the woods. Grandfather gently shook her awake right at the edge of the woods.

"Hannah, what would you like to do with the horn? You can show it to your parents or you can keep it hidden," he said, his eyes serious.

Hannah thought for a moment and then answered, "We can put it into the saddlebag to hide it. I don't want Mother or Father to see it. I don't think they would believe me anyway. I'll just tell them that I stayed warm in the leaves."

Grandfather winked at Hannah and carefully took the horn from her hands. As cautiously as he could, he wrapped it in a spare blanket and then placed it into the saddle bag. Hannah sighed and Grandfather looked at her, "Don't be sad Hannah. You know that they are real and that's all that matters."

Hannah smiled at him and answered, "I guess you're right. Let's go! I want to see my mother and father."

Grandfather chuckled at her enthusiasm and urged Dandy into a canter as they broke through the woods into the yard of Hannah's house.

"Mother! Father!" Hannah yelled joyfully when she saw them run out of the house.

"Oh Hannah!" her mother cried. Grandfather lifted Hannah off Dandy and she wasted no time running to her mother, who gathered her up in her arms, tears falling from her eyes. Her father ran up to join them and wrapped his arms around both, his normally dry eyes welling up in tears.

"We thought we lost you forever," Father said.

"I didn't think I would ever see you again," Hannah sobbed.

They stood there for a moment in that embrace, each thinking of what could have happened if Grandfather hadn't found Hannah in the woods.

Father was the first one to let go and he asked, "What happened Hannah? We got the ransom note and had the money ready to go, but no one showed up, so we assumed the worst."

"Well, I escaped from Pete and Joe and ran into the woods..."

"Pete and Joe?!" her father interrupted. Anger filled his eyes and Hannah could've sword she saw steam come out of his ears.

"Those scumbags! I fired them for stealing money so they kidnapped my daughter?!"

"Steven!" Hannah's mother exclaimed. "You don't need to use such language around Hannah! Besides, you interrupted her story."

"It's okay Mother," Hannah spoke up. "They are scumbags."

Father laughed at her and Mother shushed her for using such language.

"Well," Father said. "I'm sorry for interrupting your story Hannah. Please go on. What happened after you escaped?"

"I ran into the woods to hide from them. They followed me for a little bit, but then I got so far away that they wouldn't be able to find me anymore."

"How did you survive the night?" Mother asked. "It's still so cold."

"I..." Hannah paused and looked at Grandfather, who nodded at her. "I hid in some leaves to keep myself warm. The sun was shining when I woke up."

"That was a very smart thing to do darling," Mother spoke softly. Her eyes were still shining with tears over her daughter.

"Oh Mother," Hannah whispered. "Don't cry anymore. I'm home now."

Mother nodded and hugged Hannah again, placing her hand on the back of her head. Hannah winced at her touch and Mother said with a quizzical look on her face, "What happened there?"

"When I was wandering through the woods trying to find my way back, I accidentally fell into the river. I must've hit my head pretty hard, because I woke up a while later up on the banks."

Father looked confused.

"How did you get out of the river?" he asked.

"Ummm...I don't really know," Hannah responded. It was the truth though. She didn't know for sure if it was Luna or her Maker that had pulled her out of the river.

"Come. Let's go get something to eat," Mother said as she took Hannah's hand and led her into the house. Father walked on the other side of Mother and Grandfather took Hannah's other hand.

Later that night, after Hannah had been tucked into bed and kissed multiple times, she tiptoed across her bedroom floor and slowly opened the door. Grandfather had promised to bring Luna's horn to her after everyone else had gone to sleep that night. She waited patiently for him in her open doorway. Finally, when she could barely stand to wait any longer, Grandfather's footsteps sounded on the stairs. Hannah saw his head bobbing as he made his way up to the second floor. Her heart beating in her chest, she noticed the wrapped package in his hand. Grandfather had taken off the blanket and had rolled Luna's horn in a piece of white leather tied with a blue ribbon. Hannah reached out her hands to take the package Grandfather presented to her. He winked at her and she hugged him goodnight before retreating back into her room, shutting the door behind her.

Her hands were trembling as she untied the blue ribbon and unrolled the soft white leather, revealing the unicorn horn. Its beauty took her breath away and all of the memories from the past couple days came rushing back at her. She remembered the night that Luna had curled up next to her, she remembered how safe she had felt walking through the woods on her back, and she remembered her sacrifice to protect the one she had chosen.

Still clutching the horn in her hand, Hannah walked over to her window and slowly pushed it open. Her eyes wandered up to the heavens, drinking in the light of the stars and moon. She knew that Luna was up there with her Maker, watching over her and she was safe.

Hannah rolled the horn back up into the leather and secured the ribbon around it once more. Then, moving slowly as if to honor Luna's memory, Hannah knelt down in front of her cedar chest, lifted the lid, and popped open the secret compartment. She carefully placed the horn into the chest and took out the beautiful journal she had gotten for her birthday. She spent the majority of the night writing down her adventure in the woods with Luna and the Sephramin people. On the last page of the book, she wrote down Soo-shani's last words to her before they left.

⚬

Never forget, dear one, you are a chosen one of the stars.
Once chosen by a star, you are chosen forever.
Luna and her Maker, along with all her brothers
and sisters will be watching over you forever.
Do not walk in fear, but walk in strength, love, and peace.
Honor Luna's memory, but don't let your heart be troubled

⚬

YEARS LATER...

Hannah knew she was dying. She could feel her life slowly slipping away, and there was no coming back around for her this time. In her heart, there was peace, but she needed to see her daughter, Lily first. After Hannah died, she wouldn't have any parents left since her father had died at sea a few years back. Her grandfather would be the one to take care of her from now on. Hannah rang the little bell that her maid, Minnie had given her if she needed anything. Minnie's smiling face appeared in the doorway moments later, ready for anything.

"Minnie, please bring me my daughter," Hannah requested.

"Yes milady," Minnie replied before turning back down the stairs.

A short time later, Hannah's 9-year-old daughter Lily peeked her head around the doorpost into her mother's bedroom.

"Yes Mother?" Lily asked.

"Lily, my love. Come in so I can see you," Hannah spoke, her voice cracking.

Lily walked into the room, revealing a soiled dress and muddy shoes, her eyes looking a bit mischievous as she looked around the room.

"Lily, were you out with Lucas again?" Hannah asked, not surprised at all.

"Maybe..." Lily replied, grinning at her mother. "We raced down the big hill behind his house and I won!"

Hannah chuckled at her daughter and motioned for her to come closer. Mother and daughter had the same eyes, but Lily had dark brown hair that fell past her waist. It was normally tied into a braid to keep it away from her face, but it must have come loose during her antics with her best friend.

"Lily, we need to talk about some very important things," Hannah began. Lily's joyful eyes took on a more serious tone.

"What's wrong Mother?" Lily asked.

"I'm dying my love," Hannah said softly. "I know that I don't have much time left and I want to make sure that you are going to be okay."

Lily's eyes filled with tears at her mother's words.

"No. You're going to get better. You have to get better. Who will play unicorns with me Mother? Lucas doesn't like girly things and Grandfather doesn't believe in them. You can't leave me."

Hannah's heart twisted at her daughter's desperate words, but there was nothing she could do.

"I'm so sorry Lily," Hannah spoke with tears in her eyes. "I never wanted to leave you, but this is beyond my control. If there was something I could do to help it, I would. I have something to give to you though."

Hannah reached under her pillow and pulled out the key to her cedar chest in the attic. She handed it to Lily and said, "If you ever need an adventure, go to my cedar chest in the attic. But remember, there is more to it than meets the eye."

Hannah finished her sentence as a coughing fit began racking her body. Lily crawled into the bed with her and clung to her as she cried. Hannah wrapped her arms around her daughter, comforting her in her final hour.

Minnie came back into the room at the sound of Hannah's coughing and escorted Lily out. When they were gone, Hannah heard a sound from afar. It was distant and strange, yet so familiar. Her eyes fluttered shut as the sound came again. This time, it was closer. The memory of her fall in the river rushed back as she identified where the sound had come from. It was the whistle that Luna's Maker had made when He came to save her from the darkness. The living darkness surrounded her again in her dream, but this time she wasn't afraid of it. She knew that the Maker was coming for her. The ball of light appeared again, but this time, it transformed into a man. The same man that had come for Luna. His smile and laughing eyes were so familiar to Hannah that all her fears for Lily and her family were erased in a single moment. He held out his hand to her and uttered one word, "Come."

Without hesitation, Hannah took his hand and rose up off the bed. He led her back the way He had come, into the light where her beloved Luna was waiting for her.

AT HER MOTHER'S FUNERAL the following week, Lily clutched the key she had given her in one hand and held her grandfather's hand in the other. There were no more tears left for her to cry, so she just stood there, watching the priest conduct the ceremony. When the funeral was over, her best friend, Lucas, came up and gave her a hug. She clung to him even though her mother would've said that it wasn't proper to hug a boy like that. He was one year older than she was and used it to his advantage most of the time, but not now.

"If you need anything, I am always there for you Lily," Lucas said sympathetically.

Lily nodded her head and wiped away the tears from her eyes.

"Thank you Lucas. I just need you to be my friend forever. You can't ever leave me, okay?"

He nodded his head and smiled slightly, "I promise, we will be friends forever."

Back at her grandfather's house that night, Lily was sitting on her bed, turning her mother's key over and over in her hand. She had never been allowed in the attic because there were breakable things up there, and she had never been a graceful child. Making up her mind, Lily crept out of her bedroom door to the stairs. Everyone else was asleep, so Lily had no trouble sneaking up to the attic. Lily could barely see anything in the darkness, but there was one trunk that stood out to her. It was a dark brown cedar chest with carved swirls across the bottom. The smooth lid reflected the moonlight streaming through the skylight window above her. Lily made her way over to the trunk and knelt down beside it. Then slowly, she placed the key into the keyhole of the chest. Cautiously, she turned the key until it clicked and lifted the lid, her mind racing with what wonders she might find in her mother's chest.

www.ingramcontent.com/pod-product-compliance
Lightning Source LLC
Chambersburg PA
CBHW072112150726
47999CB00005B/2008